THE
WIZARD
OF PRALI

THE WIZARD OF PRALI

By

Davidson L. Haworth

iUniverse, Inc.
Bloomington

The Wizard Of Prali

Copyright © 2011 by Davidson L. Haworth.

All rights reserved. No part of this book may be used or reproduced by any means, graphic, electronic, or mechanical, including photocopying, recording, taping or by any information storage retrieval system without the written permission of the publisher except in the case of brief quotations embodied in critical articles and reviews.

iUniverse books may be ordered through booksellers or by contacting:

iUniverse
1663 Liberty Drive
Bloomington, IN 47403
www.iuniverse.com
1-800-Authors (1-800-288-4677)

Because of the dynamic nature of the Internet, any web addresses or links contained in this book may have changed since publication and may no longer be valid. The views expressed in this work are solely those of the author and do not necessarily reflect the views of the publisher, and the publisher hereby disclaims any responsibility for them.

Any people depicted in stock imagery provided by Thinkstock are models, and such images are being used for illustrative purposes only.
Certain stock imagery © Thinkstock.

ISBN: 978-1-4620-5535-7 (sc)
ISBN: 978-1-4620-5536-4 (hc)
ISBN: 978-1-4620-5537-1 (ebk)

Library of Congress Control Number: 2011916852

Printed in the United States of America

iUniverse rev. date: 09/14/2011

Dedicated to my love
Marina

CHAPTER 1

The Wizard and the Saint

A cold winter's night on the first night of the winter solstice deep within the Italian mountains, a dark secret lies. Tonight there is no moon. Dark clouds of winter cover the sky. Mist and snow embrace the mountain side. Tonight an ancient secret will be revealed. Inside the mountain a hidden church shines, rays of golden light peering from the moss covered entry. A diminutive cave entry to the church on the mountain side barely noticed by the human eye and within a region of treacherous mountains which lies adjacent to the French border and an environment of mystery and mysticism, a place of legends. Standing before the entry of the mountain cave; a lone figure with a flowing white robe, his face angelic untouched by age. His head shaved and his skin pale as the moonlight. He is the light this night. The lone figure turns to a small child who wears rags and the look of a pauper. The man speaks to the child who now hides in the dark cold winter shadows of the mountain side.

"My boy, do not be afraid. The evil that resides within the cave will be extinguished. Patience must be absolute." The boy smiles towards the angelic figure before him while walking towards the robed man, remaining by his side. The boy speaks softly to the man.

"Father will we set free the church for the people to worship and enter the church after this night?" The man patted the boy on the head lightly, like a parent to their child. "Yes we shall make our church free from this pestilence once and for all." The man motions his hand towards large boulders adjacent to the cave entry. The boy remembering the orders with the motion of the Fathers hand, runs towards the boulders and makes himself hidden to the world. Only an expert would be able to find the boys hiding place. Only he and the father will know, the boy laying low, breathing slowly, trying remaining calm, his eyes showing worry and nervousness.

The man in white slowly moves towards the lighted opening of the cave, his walking stick in hand, a concealed weapon beneath his robes. The shape of the weapon outlined under the garment while the man walks cautiously towards the ominous entry his mind focused on the mission that must be faced. The bright golden light glaring upon the robed figures face as he enters the cave with reservation and cautiousness the ultimate challenge awaits. Within the cave a golden church, the height from the floor to the cave ceiling reached one hundred and fifty feet high. The width of the cave seems just as large. The man in white searches the large room with his eyes. His confidence in his demeanor shows that he knew the cave well and knew what he was searching for. To his left he notices the small prayer room lit with fragranced candles and silhouettes of saintly statues. To his right the long walk way towards an altar on the other side of the mountain church. He slowly walks towards the altar, his eyes squinting, noticing another figure on the other side of the room, a figure standing firm and resolute in front of the altar. The man in white walks towards the ominous figure, his pace relaxed and confident, though tempted to reach for the hilt of his sword. He now finds himself before the figure and the altar. The man before the altar is dressed in a long flowing robe adorned in the color of royalty, purple. The cuffs and hood black as night, his beard white as snow, and his face marred with age.

The old man in purple lifts the hood from his head and sneers towards the man in white, his voice ancient and impetuous. "You have returned Bernard; you have no place in this church of the mountain and it is transformed by my rule. I control its sanctum." Bernard responds to the old man." Well Simon Magnus. You have lived a long life, only given to you by the powers of hell. So long ago has it been. The day you were cast down by the apostles. You played with black magic. You tried to retain power for yourself and not for the kingdom. You came from the city Samaritan, but fell from grace when you called yourself the great power of God. You only gained fame by becoming the first heretic. You now serve Satan. You are his agent. You study black arts, and use it to benefit your own wants and needs. Today I will take back this church in the mountain. The church I built for the people of Italia."

Simon Magnus cackles, the room filling with his sinister tone. "Dear Bernard, you have no idea of the power I hold. I sold my soul, and for it I have gained great power. Power has retained this church for my mutation experiments upon the people of this region and eventually the entire world and to the heavens beyond I am the new alpha and omega. Soon they will follow me and I will become the true earthly power." Bernard looks deep into the eyes of Simon Magnus. "This is my domain Magnus! I built this church, and it stays in my power! "Simon continues to laugh and says. "Over my dead body Priest!"

A purple glow forms around the elderly hands of Magnus his body quivers slightly. Moving his hands to his face he breathes into the glowing light forming around his hands. The color grows in strength, the purple color growing darker. A tight glowing ball now formed around his hands, his eyes glowing red. He looks up towards Bernard and smiles. "Time to die . . . . " Magnus throws the glowing orb towards Bernard with great speed and strength. The priest is shocked with the attack, and is unprepared. The glowing ball striking the priest, his body is surrounded by the purple glow and is thrown against the wall of the underground church; Bernard's body feels the sting of the wall, the sound of the wall cracking, mixed with the loud thud of the priest's body. Bernard falls to the ground, motionless. Simon Magnus smiles in evil delight, looking down at the priest. Magnus mocks the helpless Bernard. "You are no match for Magnus. The apostles under estimated me, and now you do the same. They are dead, and now so you will be." Magnus turns towards the altar to retrieve his book of black magic. Suddenly Bernard moves his arms, and lifts himself up from the ground. Dust and pieces of rock fall to the ground from his body. The priest rips his robe from his body with his left hand, his garment drifting to the ground of the cave. The priest now revealing his black tunic with a meager looking sword at his side and his eyes focus on the enemy before him his heart beating like a drum. Taking the sword from its sheath he challenges Magnus. "Magnus it is time for you to be put in your place!" With those words Bernard charges the Heretic, sword in hand.

Simon Magnus turns to face Bernard with a look of delight, and responds. "Ah now I must kill you and send you back to God!" Magnus raising his hands shoulder level, palms facing Bernard. He only laughs, while Bernard charges forward. Orange beams of light shoot from both palms of Magnus. He sneers and says. "How about a little dragon breathe dead man!" Bernard moving forward sees the orange light originating from the hands of his enemy. He jumps over the beams, and rolls to the ground. The room grows darker, the beams departing back into the hands of Magnus. The priest stands before him. "You have lived many years. In this time you have been defeated by the saints. Now you shall be defeated once more!" The eyes of Magus grow colder, and a darker red consumes his pupils. From the hands of Magnus small arrows of light shoot from under his elderly finger nails. Bernard noticing the little darts moves back and forth, dodging his enemies attack. Magnus growing impatient creates a fist with both his hands and launches an icy blue light towards Bernard. The priest takes his sword and holds the hilt with both hands before him. With all his strength he holds tight to his weapon. The blue light rushes towards Bernard, hitting his sword. The sword pulls the blue energy from Magnus within itself and soaks up the power of the wizard and defusing the attack of the powerful robed figure, the power drains to nothingness and an empty attack, the sword prevailing. He ceases his attack while the sword of Bernard glows icy blue. Raising the sword, and lifting his defiant chin towards Magnus. The monk says. "Magnus you recognize this sword? You should, you have seen it before. It is the sword of Peter, and handed down to Clement of Rome and every successor since Peter. This is Peter's sword. Now you shall perish by this sword once again!"

Simon's eyes grow in fear. His red eyes turn back to their natural color of pale blue. The evil wizard of darkness takes two steps backwards. He realizes he underestimated the priest. He did not expect an average priest to be carrying the sword of Popes. Before Simon Magnus can speak, or brace himself against an attack. Bernard swings the sword like a bat. The blue light surrounding the sword releases itself and launches towards Magnus. With lightning speed the light hits Simon Magnus squarely in the chest, his body flying into the wall behind the altar, the pain searing through his bones. His body begins to curl in agony. "You bastard priest you will die for this!" Magnus cries out, the blue energy surrounds Magnus, as Bernard looks on. Suddenly the energy cuffs the hands of Magnus to the wall, then his feet. Blue ice begins to form, over taking the body of Magnus. The ice creeps its way towards the head of Magnus covering his body while he screams in anger and defeat, the hate flowing within him more and more. "I shall return!!" He gargles with his last breath, the ice finally overtaking his body. Simon Magnus the first heretic is now encased in a tomb of ice. Never shall he wreak havoc on the people of Prali or the Turin province again. Bernard takes the sword and returns it to his belt.

Turning away from the encased wizard with a sense of a clear victory and security, he pauses and then returns his eyes towards the defeated wizard once more to face his enemy for the last time. With a gleam in his eye he chants an ancient prayer, the prayer of

Saint Michael. "O Glorious Prince of the heavenly host, St. Michael the Archangel, defend us in the battle and in the terrible warfare that we are waging against the principalities and powers, against the rulers of this world of darkness, against the evil spirits. Come to the aid of man, whom Almighty God created immortal, made in His own image and likeness, and redeemed at a great price from the tyranny of Satan. Fight this day the battle of the Lord, together with the holy angels, as already thou hast fought the leader of the proud angels, Lucifer, and his apostate host, who were powerless to resist thee, nor was there place for them any longer in Heaven. That cruel, ancient serpent, who is called the devil or Satan who seduces the whole world, was cast into the abyss with his angels. Behold this primeval enemy and slayer of men has taken courage. Transformed into an angel of light, he wanders about with all the multitude of wicked spirits, invading the earth in order to blot out the name of God and of His Christ, to seize upon, slay and cast into eternal perdition souls destined for the crown of eternal glory. This wicked dragon pours out, as a most impure flood, the venom of his malice on men of depraved mind and corrupt heart, the spirit of lying, of impiety, of blasphemy, and the pestilent breath of impurity, and of every vice and iniquity."

Taking his hand and raising it to the heavens he continues the prayer. "These most crafty enemies have filled and inebriated with gall and bitterness the Church, the spouse of the immaculate Lamb, and have laid impious hands on her most sacred possessions. In the Holy Place itself, where the See of Holy Peter and the Chair of Truth has been set up as the light of the world, they have raised the throne of their abominable impiety, with the iniquitous design that when the Pastor has been struck, the sheep may be. Arise then, O invincible Prince, bring help against the attacks of the lost spirits to the people of God, and give them the victory. They venerate thee as their protector and patron; in thee holy Church glories as her defense against the malicious power of hell; to thee has God entrusted the souls of men to be established in heavenly beatitude. Oh, pray to the God of peace that He may put Satan under our feet, so far conquered that he may no longer be able to hold men in captivity and harm the Church. Offer our prayers in the sight of the Most High, so that they may quickly find mercy in the sight of the Lord; and vanquishing the dragon, the ancient serpent, who is the devil and Satan, do thou again make him captive in the abyss, that he may no longer seduce the nations. Amen." Once amen was said the ice began to strengthen, crushing the body of Magnus into perpetual prison of ice, the prayer being the final lock to his imprisonment. Only a prayer from evil could ever release this prince of dark wizardry.

The little boy, who was ordered to stay outside, walks into the cave cautiously. He found Bernard observing the encased wizard. Tugging on Bernard, the child looks up towards the mystical priest. "Did you win father? Is the evil gone?" Bernard pats the child on the head in an act of consolation. "He is gone my son, never to return to us in this lifetime. He has created pain and suffering through the ages. He has been defeated." Bernard takes the hand of the child and proceeds to walk him back outside. The church in the cave is safe once again. No longer will evil reign here. Bernard and the child walk out of the cave, looking onwards towards the Prali region some distance below. Taking in a deep breath, the fresh air filling the lungs of the priest, a smile comes upon his face. "You are free my child. Now go and tell everyone it is time to worship once more in my church. The child releases the priest's hand, and runs down the steep trail leading to the villages. Bernard looks onward, the sun beating against his face, thinking of his mission near the French Italian mountain side. In his mind Bernard dreams of going back home to Burgundy to visit his large family of brothers and sisters. His mother dying at age nineteen brought him grief, and he prayed for her soul for years. Bending to his knees he looks up towards the sun and begins to speak.

"Dear holy mother. How I dream of the day I can return to solitude, and read nothing but great literature. How I desire to spend my life reading the classics. Instead I am here in Italy doing your bidding." In his mind a voice came to him, a female voice. "Return to Clairvaux, Your duty is done here." Bernard in silence lifts himself from his bended position, clutching his rosaries, blowing a kiss towards the heavens. Bernard slowly turns and looks back towards the church door hidden behind the rocks. A moment of silence overtook his mind; the encased wizard he had destroyed left his mind for a moment. The mission of Simon Magnus is no more. A new day has dawned. Inside the cave this Simon Magnus remains. Decades pass, nothing disturbed his sleep. From time to time he would hear voices, and sounds, people speaking of chanting; spells and the sound of a dragon, a battle taken place before him. He could not see, he could not think. Just glimpses of sounds surrounding him. From time to time he would hear something, or a thought would miraculously appear in his mind. Nothing more, there was no concept of time, everything in the world standing still for Simon Magnus.

The cavernous church thrived for years. The people would come and worship. Through the years the attendance would diminish. Till one day the people would forget of the church among the mountains. Several earthquakes and volcanic eruptions arose through time eliminated the main entryways into the church. Soon time would take its course. Rocks and moss, plant life, would cover the church. Eventually it would only be spoken of in legends. The priest who defeated Magnus would eventually die; and his battle with Magnus would be forgotten, only remembered in secret documents within the Vatican walls, never to be released till the second coming of Christ. The Vatican eventually would forget all the events and in the end only remember the location by its name, Saint Bernard's pass. Eventually the priest who encased Magnus would become a Saint, and the pass would be named after him. Many wars and political changes occurred, Many Popes come and go. Places like Turin would become popular. New orders formed. Things change, and most of the past gone. Generation after generation passed. It is a new day. Now the events and the church is a forgotten history . . . .

CHAPTER 2

Devastation and Forgiveness

Prali Italy—A young girl surrounded by clothes, her hands moving up and down in the riverbed. "One, two, three, rinse." The girl abhors laundry it is not her favorite of the daily chores. The girl is seventeen years of age her complexion fair, she has the look of innocents, clothes worn and unkempt, she continues to wash. "One, two, three, rinse." A gleam of sweat appearing on her brow, catching her breath she says. "Mother can I take a break?" The girl shouting to another woman not far from the river, the girl waits for an answer, none was given. Turning around she notices her mother is nowhere to be seen. Standing from her knees, she throws the shirt she just washed into the river. Her face red with anger and dismay, the look of frustration shows upon her face. "Why me Lord!" The girl yells. Not a word came from the sky while she looks up to the heavens waiting for an answer to her question. Suddenly the girl hears a squeaky young voice behind her. "Miss Mary Archer. Your mother left you out to dry once again?" With a hint of laughter the voice originating from a friend of the girl, while the girl named Mary turns to her friend and responds in anger. "Annalisa only you would creep on me and startle me. Why don't you do me a favor and help with these clothes?" The adorable Annalisa looks at Mary and says. "No thank you. I am headed to Lacopo's home to lie in the sun and allow him to hold me in the wheat fields." Annalisa smirked and continued. "You know Mary. You should find yourself a man. You are getting old." A slight chuckle escapes her lips. Mary responds in her typical English accent. "You know Italian men are total and complete rubbish. I want no part of it." Speaking while she dries her hands upon her blue and white dress, Annalisa looks at Mary up and down knowing that she did not think kindly of her kin folk, knowing her friend has kept to herself these many days after the rebuilding of their town. "Well I think no Italian man would want a girl who sits and works all day. Look at you, you're a mess. You need to stay fresh and clean, splash rose petal scented oils on your body. You need to find a man who will honor you and take care of you." Mary not appreciating her friend's advice responds. "When I return home to England I shall." Annalisa looked at the road ahead. "Good luck Mary. You will be with us for a long time. Now if you don't mind I'm going to see Lacopo before his mother gets back from Turin." Annalisa with those words leaves Mary surrounded by laundry. Mary speaking under her breath with a slight distain towards her friend and the frustration of the disappearance of her mother who seems to have left Mary by her lonesome with enough laundry to make the most experienced washer faint in agony. "Typical fourteen year olds," Mary says under her breath, while she looks down towards the ground.

Mary looks up and down the river, the adjacent meadow, her mother has gone. Mary waits for hours until the sun began to set behind the mountains. She looked towards the mountains and remembers her adventure two years ago. The day Bernard and herself slayed the dragon in the mountain pass of Saint Bernard and the dangers that came to them during their journey, remembering her friend who perished on their quest. It seems so distant, and yet so close, she picks up her laundry and heads home. The young girl realizing her mother is not at home waits patiently for her return. Another startle for Mary hearing a slight knock upon her door, a rare event since her and her mother kept to their own. Mary brushes her hands against her blouse then slowly heads fir the door, placing her hand on the door knob, turning it slowly. A creaking sound emanates from the old door hinges. A man from the town center stands before her in full uniform, she recognizes him as the town mayor. Mary smiles and says. "Hello sir, would you like to enter. This is a pleasant surprise indeed." The mayor enters with a somber look upon him. Upon entering he asks Mary. "May I have a seat by the fire?" Mary smiles and pulls out a chair for the man. "Here sir please sit and make yourself comfortable, you are always welcome in the house of my mother. What gives us the pleasure of your visit?" Mary asked sheepishly. The man almost coming to tears looks at Mary and says. "Please sit down I have something I need to say." Mary's heart fell. Thoughts came to her mind, grim thoughts. Images of the worse possibilities come to her mind. She nervously sits unhinged, waiting for his the words to escape his lips.

The mayor sat in the chair, uncomfortable and unable to speak. Eventually with a thought of how he will present the news to Mary, he spoke. "My dear Mary I have grave news in regards to your mother." Mary hearing the words "grave news" brought her to tears. The lump in her throat slowly begins to form, finding it hard to swallow. The sparkle of her eyes fades in the firelight, a tear forms and falls upon her cheek while despair and grief came to her soul, a feeling of great sorrow, numbness came to invade her senses. The mayor needed to say no more. Mary knew now what the remainder of the news will be. She sat in sorrow and waited for the Mayor to continue. "She passed away my dear, blindsided by a knight on his horse. We arrested the knight for being drunk and killing your mother. Many people witnessed this event. He will be sentenced and sent to death." Mary clutches her hands against the armchair, suddenly she falls to the ground in agony, crying without restraint, the mayor kneeling before her doing his best to comfort the young girl from the grave news that befell the young girl and the life this girl must now endure without family. Mary lost all thoughts of anything around her, eventually passing out. The mayor in his gentleman duty picked her up and carried her to her bedroom. Lifting the covers from the bed, placing her under the covers making sure the girl will be comforted in her anguish, he says. "Rest easy my dear. Justice will be served."

A week passes in the Turin region, one week of misery for the young Mary in Prali, standing before her mother's gravestone, her eyes red from crying, her arms shivering from the oncoming winter. Hearing footsteps behind her the Mayor approaches. "My girl the knight was found guilty of drunkenness and murder. He has been sentenced to death for your mother's murder. He will never kill again." Mary reaching in her pocket for her rosary, thinking of the Mayors words and responds. "My good sir I thank you for your justice, but my mother would not want it this way. If you kill the knight because of my mother's death, than how much better are we. May I make a request?" The Mayor confused, and bewildered granted Mary permission to continue with her request. "Thank you kind Mayor, I request the knight be jailed in prison for life, until he grows old and dies. We cannot have blood on our hands. My mother would agree with me. Please sir, attain for him life without ever getting out of jail. Allow him to think of what he has done every day for the rest of his life. That is a far greater punishment and torture." The Mayor nodded and said. "My lady your wish will be done. The court will grant you anything. It is as good as done." The Mayor pausing, and then asking one more question to the young girl who stared into the blankness of her surroundings, her mind filled with images of her childhood and her parents. "Will you be staying in Prali, or will you go home to your motherland of Britannia?" Biting her lower lip looking as if in deep thought, her mind spinning from the simplest of questions, preoccupied with sorrow within her and the enduring pain of losing a loved one, she is the last of the Archer clan in a world of darkness and wickedness surrounded by those who live under the stain of the human condition, mankind with the weakness of sin and depravity. "I have not decided yet good sir. I shall pray about it and leave it up to the Lord above." The Mayor bowed and walked away from Mary, back to his duty.

Mary kneels upon the cold ground, the snow falling lightly upon her sorrowful face. "Mother I know you can hear me. What shall I do? I am only seventeen and alone. Now you are with papa. I want to join you, but still I know I have work to do here. Mother I must confess to you. I never told you, but two years ago when the town of Prali was being tormented by the dragon. The day the dragon stopped appearing. Mother I was the one to slay the dragon. I had guidance with the help of Brother Bernard, who actually killed the dragon. Still I had a hand in it. I just thought you should know mother. I know you would have been proud of me, and now you know. I only wish you were here now." Mary began to cry once more. Feeling alone in the world, no one to turn to, until suddenly, "Mary you slayed the dragon of Prali?" A familiar voice originating from behind her, the same voice she heard on the last day she saw her mother alive and well. Mary turned, and standing behind her was no other than Annalisa. Mary became angry and stood from her knelt position, her hands leaning on her hips. "Annalisa how dare you listen to my conversation with my mother, who do you think you are coming into my abode and starling me in an intimate moment?" Annalisa walks toward Mary and embraces her. "I am a friend Mary." The two girls embraced, both crying for the sorrow of a deceased mother, and the confessions of a heroin.

Annalisa pulls away from Mary and asks the question once more. "Did you really kill that dragon . . . . Did you?" The look of disbelief on Annalisa's face waiting for clarification from her friend, thinking maybe her friend has become unwell mentally since the death of her mother. With a look of concern of the weighty question, Mary responds to her friends query. "Yes it is true. I had a hand in killing the dragon, but you must not tell a soul. It is a secret only Brother Bernard and I know. We lost many people on our mission, including a knight who would have swept you off your feet." Annalisa smiled and said. "This knight is gone from us?" Mary nodding her head in a confirming response. "Please keep the secret to yourself. I need to remain who I am, if you go around telling the world of what I did they may not believe me, and great harm may come, especially now that my mother is dead. The people of Prali may think I am looking for attention, the last resort of a lone girl without a family. You see, now keep things secret. Let the truth die with me." Annalisa nodding her head in agreement, saying. "Now what shall you do Mary? Everyone is talking about you and your next move." Mary walks from her mother's grave and begins to travel back to her lonely home. "I have no idea what I will do. Why does everyone wonder about what I will do next? Who cares, for now I want to be alone, maybe I will leave the ills of this world and become a Nun." Annalisa laughs and responds. "You don't join a convent because you lost something. You join because you found something. I think you need to get back to life." Mary smiles lightly and says. "Yes, life is out there somewhere, but I need to find myself first and then I will continue with my life." Annalisa found Mary becoming more comfortable the farther she walked away from the cemetery. "Mary why don't you come with me and Lacopo tonight we are going into the woods to see shooting stars and I hear there will be a bright moon as well?" Mary for the first time laughing out loud thinking how uncomfortable she will feel being a third wheel tagging along with her friend and her lover, a humorous situation since Mary wishes not think of her friends boyfriend, he is like most Italian men who drink and eat their lives away. "No Annalisa. That is for you and him. I know you do more than just look at stars. I would just be a third wheel." The two girls smiled and continued to walk. Annalisa eventually giving Mary a kind friendly embrace before departing to see Lacopo the one man who gives purpose to her young life in the small town of limited attractions, nothing in town except friends, family, church, the kind of life that most experience in a small town away from the rest of the world, better yet most of Italy.

In the evening Mary opens her door to her little cottage and looks out into the darkness. Only the flickering of candlelight within her home gives her comfort. She watches while the snowflakes glide down from the darkened skies, and onto the land. This winter looks to be the coldest. Mary shivered and thought of her life, and her future. She knew not what the future held. She prayed that it would not be cold as this night. Shutting her door she walks toward the fire and continues to think of her life, talking to herself. "I feel like a loser. I have nothing, only this small home. No family and a couple of friends. I wonder if England is calling me home. Life seems to pass me by. Do I have a purpose? I have always been told I do have one, I just don't see it." Mary feeling her eyes heavy and weakened, closing her eyes falling asleep by the firelight. Through the night the fire keeps her warm and snug. Her only solace was in sleep. She abhors being awake, it brings memories and sadness. She could dream forever.

The next morning Mary woke to the rooster call, rubbing her eyes, the fire smoldering, with only embers to be seen. Rising from the chair she walks over to the window. The window was covered in ice. She decides to open the door, to her surprise the snow has arrived early this winter. Two feet of snow already on the ground and more to come, it was becoming a winter to remember. Mary never liked winters in Prali. To be barricaded in your home for most of the time is not her idea of fun. Mary started her day with a morning scrub, then a walk to the barn to fetch goat's milk and eggs. In the barn she began to place eggs in her basket. Then a pain in her chest formed, sorrow returned to her once more, her mind reenacting the events of her father, then her mother's death. Falling to the ground, leaning upon the hens cage she begins to cry once more. "Please take this pain away!!" She cries out. Mary realizes she will never mend this heart, only to live the rest of her days in sorrow. Eventually she regains her composure, and lifts herself from the ground, wiping away her tears, placing the eggs in the basket. Looking around the barn she wonders what life is all about. She knew where to find the answer; it is in the monastery above the town in the hills. Mary runs back to her cottage and places her best dress upon her body. In the snow she walks through town and up the hill to the Franciscan monastery. Knocking on the door, a young brother answers with a confused look upon his face, not expecting a young girl to be bothering the brothers during prayers and reflection, a time to think of ones relationship with the almighty and the brothers who died on the fateful day of the dragon where many died. "Yes my lady may I help you?" His calm words soothed Mary from the start. "Yes brother you may be of assistance. I am looking for Brother Bernard. I am a friend of his and I need his guidance on a certain issue." The brother smiles at Mary and says. "I'm sorry my lady. Bernard is now in Rome. He is in study, and may never come back to Prali." A frown appears on Mary's face. She lost everything, now she lost the one man she can turn to. The one who helped slay the dragon two years ago. The brother noticed her sorrow and said. "Is there anything I or the fathers can do for you?" Her head bowing to her chest simply says. "No." Mary turned from the brother in a daze and starts walking home with her head down. She walked ignoring all in her path. The people in Prali noticed her began to fear for her, and rumors began to circulate. Arriving at her home she fell upon her bed and cried.

The next morning Mary walked in hope for some fresh morning air through the first winters blessing of snow and cool breezes. The snow had ceased, the sun peering through the clouds, the cold chills gone for now. She walked and walked until finding herself at the top of a mountain. She looks over the town of Prali, and the mountain range, the sun beating on her face, moving her head back to feel the heat emanating from the warmth above. Taking deep breaths she spoke to herself once more. "It's time to stop. It's time to come back to life. I have mourned too long. I love my parents, now I must live for me. I need to make sure my life is secure. I will return to my homeland and start anew." Closing her eyes, and in deep thought, she smiles. She realizes it is now time to move from Prali and return to Lancashire, England. There was nothing for her now in Prali. Mary stood and watched the birds overhead, the melting snow falling from the pine trees; she knows she will miss the town of Prali. Walking back to her cottage, her plan of going back to England invaded her mind. It made her excited, another adventure, and time to return to her roots.

While Mary dreamed of her new life, Annalisa strolled through the town center of Prali with her boyfriend Lacopo. Holding hands and enjoying the sun, the snow melting below their feet. Lacopo did not act his usual energetic self. The skinny Italian boy who charmed Annalisa, and made her his for all times, how he loved her and cherished her. She smiled constantly in his presence being the happiest girl in Prali. Lacopo was nervous and unsteady the entire afternoon, Annalisa knew he needed to get something off his chest. Lacopo whispered in her ear, while people passed by them carrying their groceries and wares, while children ran under their clasped hands. Lifting their hands together to allow the children through, the streets of Prali bustling for preparations of winter and the residence stocking up on supplies, winter was always a trying time for a town nestled high upon the Italian mountain range. Lacopo looks towards his girl and says. "Come with me I need to say something." With a smile Annalisa obeyed. The two lovers running through town center, to finally rest on the edge of town. Lacopo wanted peace, and not the ramblings of the town center to speak to Annalisa. With an exhausted tone he simply fell to his knees, pulling out a simple ring. "Annalisa. Will you be my betrothed?" She smiles, a tear coming to her eye. With a warm embrace and a whisper in his ear "Yes I will marry you, and love you forever." The two young lovers stood in silence holding one another, the snow once again falling and landing upon their shoulders. They kiss, feeling their hearts beat as one. His fingers running through her hair, her arms wrapped around him.

A loud banging woke Mary the next morning, a loud voice being heard. "Mary!! Mary!! Open the door please!!" Mary not in the best of morning moods opens the door to a smiling Annalisa, her face flushed as the absent sun on this morning. Annalisa rushes into the cottage and spinning around gave Mary the great news. "I am engaged! Can you believe it Mary?" Mary standing in silence, then turning her back to her friend not pleased with the news and thinking how young her friend is and how marriage is not always a pleasant experience. "I am happy for you. I hope you get everything you want in life." Mary holding herself back from crying. "Why are you sad Mary?" Annalisa questions. "I am not sad my friend. I am truly happy for you. I have news for you also. I am going back to England. There is nothing for me here. You have it all, I have nothing. I will blaze my own trail." Annalisa shocked with the news spoke in kind. "Mary I understand what you are going through. Will you stay for the wedding? You know you may find a man and you may change your mind." Mary scoffs at the words of her friend. "Me? Please are you joking? You know how I feel about Italian men. Nothing but rubbish I tell ya." Annalisa protests. "You are rubbish Mary. Lacopo is attractive, charming, and financially secure." Mary laughs. "You must be kidding. Money is nothing. You marry for money, it will only bring you sorrow in the end. I know you are getting married for love. Money is not an issue. Let's face it attractiveness is in the eyes of the beholder, and your man is not attractive. He is nothing more than a basic Italian." Annalisa grew upset with Mary and stormed towards the door. "I came here to share news. Now I understand you are jealous of my love for him. Forget the invitation Mary. Go back to your precious England and never return!" Leaving the cottage in anger, Annalisa slams the door and leaves. Mary stands awe struck, and saddened. Seems Mary can do nothing right. She destroys everything she touches. Now her only friend is gone. Mary looks around her cottage and knows she must leave before weeks end.

Suddenly Mary's instincts took hold. She is lured to her front door. Something in her mind told her to look up towards Saint Bernard's pass. The same pass where she fought the dragon two years earlier. The snow no longer falling upon the ground and the sun returning briefly to shine upon the girl's face, clouds parting to reveal the delicate rays of precious light, she turns towards the mountain, her cheeks red with cold. In the distance she notices a flicker of light upon the mountain, barely visible, the sleet and clouds return once more to block her view. Mary realizes this means only one thing. The volcano is erupting. Living near an active volcano always bothered Mary and at times dreams of Pompeii filled her mind, she wished not for another tragic world event such as Pompeii, although the volcano never posed a threat, still the worries lingered in her mind. Observing the mountain pass, she wonders about the dead dragon. The bones are no more, mixed with the molten lava possibly rising from the volcano. Mary watched for a long time until the glowing red flames dissipated. Mary smiles knowing it is only a flare up nothing more. "Thank goodness. Glad I won't be here for the big one." Speaking to herself while shutting the door behind her.

CHAPTER 3

The Oncoming Storm

High above Prali, rumblings were heard through the peaks and valleys of the mountain region. Saint Bernard's Pass the location of forgotten history found itself once more in the midst of another volcanic eruption. Today the eruption would soon subside, except for the heat and rumblings would possibly unleash decease among the people of the Turin province and the village of Prali. Deep within the mountain rests an imprisoned wizard, the last of the wizards. Inside the forgotten church of Saint Bernard the ground began to shake, lava seeping through the flooring, heating the historic church. Cracks becoming evident, slowly the gaps grow longer and wider. Inside the church with the imprisoned wizard are two set of bones, one set large, possibly a dinosaur to the human thought process? Except these bones were only two years of age. The creature that died in the church was recent. The other set from a human form was hidden behind the church altar. Lava from underneath the church began to seep, the ground shaking, the walls quaking, pieces of ceiling falling upon the floor with a crash, the ground lifting while the remains of the large creature began to slide down into the lava abyss, the last remains of the last dragon, destroyed by the lava, the heat devouring the remains to a molten cinder of nothingness.

Across from the dragon's remains on the other side of the church behind the altar the ice encasing of the wizard begins to crack. The lava melting the tomb of the last known wizard, the dragon remains giving way to a new era in evil, the wizard's prison melts. Suddenly the rumbling ceases, the lava loses its firm control over the damaged church. Slowly the lava seeps back to its origins. The church remains silent and still, the ground damaged, the golden walls cracked, the bones of the dragon incinerated. The encased wizard still imprisoned by the ice, cracks in the ice allowing warm air to enter the casing. The wizard's mouth moves slightly, his mind returning to conscience thought. Mumbling of words escape his cracked elderly lips. "Oh mighty Lord Satan, god of this world, god of my flesh, god of my mind, god of my inner most will. Every part of this world is within your power. You are within every part of this world. Every part of me is within your power. You are within every part of me. I am yours, whether I serve you willingly or not, for I am myself, whether I am true to myself or not. Of my own free will, I now acknowledge your abundant power of my own free will, I now present myself to You, in your service" The wizard speaking the words, the words to his master. The enemy of the world free to wreak havoc among God's people, Satan's wizard returns once more. The ice cracking, crashing to the ground, blocks of ice sliding down the church altar steps, slowly melting away into the dark cracks and crevices.

The wizard stretching out his hand, a devilish smile comes to his face. "I AM FREE!!!!!" His eyes red, filled with revenge and hate. The wizards delight becomes infectious with madness. His laughs fill the cavernous church. "The apostles thought they could stop me. Pope Clement of Rome thought he could stop me. That ridiculous priest Bernard thought he could stop me. NOTHING CAN STOP SIMON MAGNUS!!!!!" The echoes of his voice vibrating in a deafening tone within the cavernous ancient church and an era of past evil has returned to lay claim upon the masses. Stretching his arms and legs from his long slumber, he notices a pile of human remains. Walking over, and bending down. Taking one of the bones in his hands, he wonders who this sad soul could be. Closing his old and tired eyes, he scans the bone with his hand. In his mind he could see what had caused the bones to be placed here in the church. Visions of a sinister creature battling a monk and his young female companion, a monk with a sword, and the girl who preferred bow and arrows, the poor creature didn't stand a chance. Suddenly the wizard became still while he gathered information in his vision. The sword, he recognized the sword held by the monk, "Ah the sword of Peter. This monk has the sword." He grew a devilish smile upon his withered face, laughing again, "This monk and this sweet girl. They killed this poor creature." Magnus opened his eyes, standing before the bones. His hand placed on his chin, while he thought "My lucky day!" laughing and thinking of evil deeds he plans on the local inhabitants and eventually the world.

Magnus placing his withered hands together, closing his eyes and looking down towards the bones, an orange glow emanating from his hands, the bones being surrounded by the magic of Magnus, and the first deed of evil to be released since his imprisonment. "This creature once served dragons, his life taken by a monk and a girl, they cheated him. Now he will serve me, and together we will wreak revenge upon the people. I am their god now. I am the ultimate salvation. The apostles spite me, now I will spite them and their church on earth." Magnus placing his palms outward towards the bones even closer, the glow becoming brighter and completely devouring the remains in its evil magic, the eyes of Magnus continues to focus on the task in hand, his mind filled with evil and revenge. Suddenly the remains begin to move, the bones connecting to each other. Simon smiles and says, "Rise!! Rise!! My servant of salvation, come to your master and be fulfilled in all knowledge of pure power." The joints mend, flesh begins to form upon the bones, building to form the resemblance of a human; Skin, hair, and teeth, a complete human now lays on the floor naked and new. "Open your eyes and live again my servant." The wizard speaking to his new found creation with an arrogant tone. The once dead man now lying naked on the floor opens his eyes. He looks up towards the wizard. Magnus smiles with his evil grin and says. "Welcome home my friend. Please tell me your name." The man on the floor amazed he is breathing responds. "My name is Skulk sir." The naked man rises from the floor looking up towards the mighty wizard. The height of Magnus hovering over the shorter man, and his nakedness brings shame upon him, he feels uneasy. "Skulk you say? I have given you a new life, raised you from the dead. I envisioned your demise, now I bring you home to serve me." Skulk feels his face, looking over his body. He smiles in disbelief. He cannot think of how amazing this wizard is. The man named Skulk, a creature of darkness and evil, now in the form of human perfection. His balding head now full and blonde, his eyes dark and soulless now blue like an ocean, his skin once withered and deceased now soft and smooth like a new born baby.

Magnus looks over his new servant and says. "I have seen your plight. I saw you in your past life. You were nothing but darkness. Now you are the perfect light to the world. You will be desired by women, and respected by men. You my friend have a new opportunity to live again." Skulk marveled hearing the words of the wizard. "Sir the only thing I remember is being struck by an arrow, and dying, then fire and pain. Demons tortured me, feeding me to the whores of Satan." Skulk bows his head and says. "I was in hell for my deeds. You saved me from hell. How can you do such a thing? Only God can do these things." Simon Magnus laughs. "I am the way and the light my friend. All you have to do is serve me and the world will be yours." Skulk fell to his knees and kissed the hand of the wizard. "I shall serve you till death. You are my master and god." Magnus lifting Skulk from his knees. "My servant we have much to do. We have a land to conquer and a sword to find. The monk you encountered has my sword. I want it back, we must find him. You will help me in this endeavor." Skulk smiles and says, "That is easy my lord. The monk was dressed in Franciscan robes. We shall find him at the monastery in Prali." Magnus places his hand upon his chin once more, looking up to the church ceiling. "Yes my servant you speak with wisdom of this province." Skulk with hate in his eyes asked the wizard for one request. "My lord I ask of you one thing. The girl who killed me, I want revenge, I want to find her and kill her." Simon Magnus closed his eyes, walking over to the area where the archer girl stood in battle, feeling the ground, probing, getting answers, feeing her invisible print upon the cave floor. With a deathly smile he says, "This girl you want. I can feel her; she is still in the region. She will be your slave. I can feel her; she will do your bidding." The wizard's face grew dark and sinister. "My dear servant you must be good in your work. You must make her suffer. I have made you perfect in the image of man. Take this girl and make her your toy, strip her of her innocents. Allow her to trust you, and then when you steal her innocents and heart, you will steal her soul and kill her in the night. Kill her once you have sinned with her. Then kill her without confession. This friend will send her to hell and allow the demons to eternally ravage her. Do this and you shall be cherished in all of hades."

Skulk smiled and said. "Yes my lord, I will use the gifts you have given me, and take this girl. Then I will get my revenge." The evil lurking within them grew and grew, with thoughts of revenge, lust, dominance, and control. Magnus closed his eyes once more; a pink glow surrounded his hands. The glow moving towards Skulk, surrounding the new human form, suddenly the color explodes around Skulk and dissipates. Skulk now standing before the wizard with new clothes. Clothes any man, woman, or child in Prali would envy. "Now you have everything you need. First we need to think of a name for thee. You cannot go around calling yourself Skulk. You are new and perfect." Simon Magnus walking around the altar in thought, thinking of a name for his servant, Skulk stands dumbfounded and thoughtless, the difference between master and servant. Magnus jumps with excitement and says. "You are no longer Skulk. You will now be named Decorus Feries. You shall only allow people to know your first name. Your last name is a spell designed to rescue you in times of need. When you spout the word Feries from your lips, three avenger demons from hell will come to you and assist you in your mission. Only in emergencies, do you understand me?

A wizard must never use his weapons unless necessary. You are no wizard or god, but you are my servant. We will avenge your death, and take the sword that belongs to me. Eventually we will destroy the Papacy and the Church of Rome. You will see my newly formed friend. Rome is the church of God. The only instrument connected to the Christ. I will destroy the church and in its place of it will be the new evolution of church. I will be the head of this church and lead it to serve me. The world will serve me and be mine. I am stronger than heaven and hell. When the apostles cast me out, it was their biggest mistake. They are all dead, and I live with the help of my deal with the master of evil. Now I will find the sword, destroy the church of the Christian God, and rule the world, nothing can stop me this time. With you at my side Decorus, nothing can go wrong. We are destined to rule over these pathetic followers. The pope's blood and all his people will be on my hands. They will be the sacrifice of the new church, the true church, with me as head." Revenge and anger in his eyes, his face of evil shown in the dark cave of Saint Bernard's Pass. "Now Decorus, let's make some magic." With a laugh he walks out of the cave with Decorus in tow.

A day has passed since the reawakened wizard regained his taste for vengeance. He and his servant stood on the edge of a small town named Briancon, not far from Prali. The wizard standing his ground wearing his purple colored cloak, his white beard withered and covered in winter frost, Decorus wearing his beautiful white tunic, and blue trousers. Magnus turns to his servant and says. "You ready to make these people our footstools?" Decorus nods with glee. The two evil doers begin their walk towards the town; an elderly lady approaches them with bag in hand. Magnus approaches the old woman and says. "Old woman where is the nearest town hall?" The woman not understanding the language of the tall man dressed in purple. She speaks to the two strangers in her local dialect, her words pleasant and kind. Simon Magnus grows with anger placing his hand upon her neck; he squeezes the life out of the old woman. Her face turning purple and blue not able to breath, Magnus lifts her from the ground, her bags drop to the icy road below. A crack of the neck is heard, her body limps. Magnus throws her into a snow bank and laughs, saying. "Looks like we lost our way, we are in France, this woman spoke French. Oh how I hate the French. Nothing good came from these lazy people. This brings me more pleasure Decorus. We have all the French we can kill here in this little town." The two strangers continue to walk through town, people observing them, Magnus ignoring the glares and stares of the locals. Placing his hand on Decorus, deep in thought, the next move? "My friend I will say this about the French. They live like the Italians. Their whole hope is in the church. Let's go to the church and see if we can make a little noise." With a sinister grin looking upwards, noticing the bell tower. "Come my servant; let's show them how this Samaritan does things."

Simon Magnus and Decorus in a matter of minutes locate the church, "Ah Saint Salome." Magnus reading the entry sign in front of the church doors. "Saint Salome. This is perfect I could not ask for anything more. This woman was mother of the apostles. How kind of me to take it over and dispose of the occupants. I think I will change the name to Saint Decorus. What do you think?" Magnus entertaining himself with his evil thoughts, Decorus liking the idea, "Yes my lord I would love to have this church named after me." Magnus patting Decorus on the head while he walks up to the doors. "Keep dreaming my servant. Keep dreaming." The wizard placed his hand on the large metal door handles of the church double doors. The large doors wooden and thick, etchings of the apostles on the door, a splendid design, inside the church a vast array of saintly statues and holy water fonts, candles lit the entire church. People prayed and meditated before the saints lighting candles. Two of the villagers felt intimidated by the wizard's presence and leaving the church through a side door.

Magnus scanned the church with his glaring eyes. The crucifix above the altar caught his eye. "Look my servant. This is the man these people serve, a dead man. I remember the day of this death and resurrection. I was a lowly Samaritan at the time. I watched his

followers perform magic tricks and great deeds. I too possessed the
same powers. They were jealous because I was better. They called
me evil and a heretic. They casted me out, now they are dead and
I continue to live through my deal with the devil. I spent years
perfecting the pagan rituals. Magic came easy to me, eventually I
became all powerful. Still these lovers of Christ still reign. Now they
will be taught their folly and know to worship the great Magnus."
The servant followed his master, both walking mightily towards the
altar.

A lone priest walks into the church and notices the two shadowy
figures standing before the altar. The priest dressed in a black
Cossack and elderly, he belonged to the Augustinian order, his duty
to serve the people of Briancon. "Excuse me kind sir may I help
you?" The priest speaking in kind, Magnus turns towards the priest,
speaking with a tone of hostility. "Do you know who I am priest? I
am Simon Magnus. You know who I am. I am in your good book.
The one targeted and made a fool of for years. Now I will destroy
your books and reclaim my name. My rule over this world will soon
come. I shall rule over Rome and the whole civilized world." The
priest backs away from Simon Magnus. Placing his rosary in his
hand, "Magnus impossible, you are dead, an outcast. How could
you live for all these years?" Magnus laughs, and replies to the priests
query. "Because my friend I am the true god." With his words came
flames from his hands, pointing his palms towards the priest. "Tell
the apostles I said hello, time to die Augustinian." A bolt of fire
blasted towards the helpless priest, the fire surrounding the priest's
body, the energy slamming the elderly body against the wall. The
villagers in the church ran for their lives, one of the men who escape
sprints to the mayor's office for help. "Now Decorus this church
needs a little redecorating, I think we should be the ones to do the
honors." The fire from Magnus ignites around his body, Decorus
runs towards the exit in fear from the wizard Magnus, the dastardly
henchman dives out the door and hides behind a tree like a child in
fear of his father, Magnus launches fire emanating from his body.

The fire spreading with a mighty force through the church like a decease, Magnus laughing with sinful pleasure, the pews in the church burning, the statues and altar ablaze, the heat fierce, causing the stone to crumble to the ground, crushing the remaining surviving pews. Decorus stepping away from the church, the snow begins to fall on the village of Briancon, smoke and flame flowing from the high church tower, the bell falling into the street. The walls crumble with great force. Rubble and fire are all that remains of the church, nothing more except the steps of the church and half of the bell tower. People from the village begin to gather to witness the shocking event. Eventually the entire town would be there to see the end of Saint Salome. Only the escaped villager and the local authorities remain unseen or hidden. The church grounds ablaze, surrounded by the magical fire, Magnus walks out from the rubble of fire, untouched and unhinged with madness. The people surrounded him in awe; Decorus stands with him in the same shock and awe. "You see my servant how easy it is to rule over these followers of this Christ. I destroy their holy place and they all come to see. Now they shall pay for their folly." Magnus winks at Decorus and continues. "Bow down before me servant and be saved from my wrath." Decorus bows to Magnus, his head against his boots. The villagers look at Magnus with anger, the body of the wizard being surrounded by a white light, another one of his magical powers. He looks at the innocent villagers, Men, Women, and Children all around him. "TIME TO SEE YOUR MAKER!!!!" he shouts to the villagers of Briancon. The French in shock witness the bright light originating from the body of Magnus. Suddenly without warning a sonic blast rockets around Magnus, Incinerating every citizen of Briancon within a one hundred foot radius. Nothing survives or remains of the people, except for the white powder on the snowy ground. All was silent; the village became dark with flying embers and ash, only Decorus survived. Magnus looks down to his servant and says. "You see my friend if those villagers would have kneeled before me like you did, they would still be alive, though I did not warn them, because I prefer them dead." Magnus lifts his servant from the ground, and brushes off the snow from his tunic.

The mayor of Briancon accompanied by twenty soldiers and the villager who escaped the church came running towards the wizard. Magnus laughs and says. "Look! These people never learn. I am their master and I will not have servants who are not loyal. They come with weapons. Not a wise choice, not a good start. Oh well you win some and lose some. Today they will lose some, and I will win. This French town belongs to Magnus." The fingertips of Magnus glow individually. Pointing his fingers towards the oncoming rush of hostile citizens, he shoots small lightning bolts shaped as arrows towards the men, the beams blazing through the winter air with the speed of light, the magic arrows penetrating every man right through the heart, their bodies falling to the ground, landing in the winter snow. "This is too easy. Let's go have some fun. Let's show the world what I am made of, time to erase this place from the history books." Magnus walking through the village with Decorus in tow, walking through the streets, he fires bolts of fire into the homes and buildings of Briancon. His eyes red with evil intentions, his body pulsing with excitement and delight, buildings burn and fall behind him while he walks. Occasionally hearing a cry for help, or the sound of death, villagers in their homes dying, the last of the citizens of Briancon. Magnus spent the day destroying the town and laughing till his mission was accomplished. Eventually finding himself atop a hill overlooking the devastation. No stone was left unturned, the entire villages gone, embers floating up towards the clouds, the snow falling upon the burnt ruins of Briancon.

CHAPTER 4

Visions and Missions

Vatican City, Italy. A cloudless night, the moon shining bright, the shadows of the statue atop the church casting images upon the walls. The stars shine above glimmering, an occasional shooting star rockets across the night. In the holy city an elderly man sleeps in his lavish bed, his hair white; body worn and slim, two Swiss guards stand at attention outside his doors. The sleeping Pope squirms in his sleep, a vision coming to him in a dream, an angel showing him the truth within his mind, reminiscent of the dreams and visions of Pope Innocent III in the time of Saint Francis of Assisi. The moon peering through the white satin curtain of his humble chambers, the window gliding around his window, his brow begins to sweat, the vision now coming into focus.

A young monk reaches for the sword and places it in his hand. He remembers that it is not just the sword that is the power but the faith of the one who carries it. The monk rushes toward the dragon with haste, hearing the death cries of his friend above his head. The monk with all his strength says a Hail Mary prayer in his mind and throws the sword of Saint Peter towards the dragon's heart, the sword flying through the air flipping around and around, the young monk watching, biting his lower lip.

The sword hits the intended target; it pierced the dragon's chest and entered his heart. The dragon releasing a loud cry from his jaws and slowly releasing his grip on Mary, the young girl falls to the ground of the cave. Her body lifeless, the monk is too late, the dragon taking his claw and holding his chest, not able to pry the sword from his evil body. Falling to the ground, landing only a few feet from the body of Mary, his tail shaking while he lays on the ground, his heart beating, and slowly dissipating, until his heart stops, movement ceasing. The mighty foe has fallen to his eternal darkness.

Pope Callistus wakes from his vision. Positioning his tired body upwards and leaning against his canopy bed headboard. The monk in his vision seemed familiar; the girl was of no consequence. He thinks long about his vision, the sword and the monk. He knew the sword well, then he realized. Two years ago a Franciscan brother brought back the sword of Saint Peter. The church gave the sword to a Swiss guard the people named Leonardo. This knight was called to vanquish the dragon and return victorious. He remembers the monk who returned the sword to the Vatican. This monk traveled far and wide to return the sword. Then the name of the province came to the Popes mind. Turin, the province of Turin. The monk came from the town of Prali. This monk never returned to the region of his origin. For his valor in returning the sword to the church from the dead knight the Vatican had sent to kill the dragon. This monk was rewarded an education within the Vatican walls. He remembered the monk joining the Franciscan college, his name was Bernard.

Pope Callistus rose from his bed and placed his red cardinal slippers upon his feet. He walks out to the window; the moon is shining on his face, the stars bright above. He thought of his vision and said. "My Lord this vision you gave me. The Franciscan, did he kill the dragon? This monk did not tell us he killed the dragon, he just returned the sword and reported the knights death." Words came to his mind, an answer to his question. "My servant, this monk slayed the dragon and returned the sword. His humility won the day and he did not inform the church of his killing the foe." The Pope walked away from the window. His hand rubbing his temple, stumbling to his prayer kneeler, placing himself in position to speak to God, looking for answers and confirmation of his dreams that intrigued him. "Why did you give me this vision, is it important that I know about this monk who killed the dragon?" The voice in his head continued to answer the Popes questions. "My servant this monk must be called to you. Our people are being slaughtered by the first heretic, the wizard Simon Magnus." His holiness the Pope in shock to hear the name of Magnus, "My Lord this Magnus is dead surely. He lived in the days of the apostles. How can this man survive all these years?" The voice continues to converse with the Pope. "My son, Magnus made a deal with Satan. In return for service Magnus was rewarded long life and powers unimaginable. Magnus adopted pagan rites. He became a wizard, a society I extinguished long ago before the recording of time of mortal man. The church has done an admirable duty eliminating the old pagan ways of wizards and elves. These creatures I created out of experiments. Once I perfected my human children I eliminated the wizards and elves. These creatures betrayed me and adopted pagan rites created by Lucifer. They embraced the pagan thought created by Satan. This thought created to compete with me and to bring these creatures into Satan's service. Humans are not perfect, there are humans who embrace the pagan thought, but they are minimal. I allow the devil to hold these people in his power. To show my people the wrong direction of faith and now Magnus has returned, He has already destroyed the village of Briancon, and is in Prali. He will not destroy Prali, he will use it to begin his religion, the religion of Magnus. You must request the monk to return to you and you must give him the sword once more. He must confront Magnus and eliminate the wizard forever."

The voice in the head of Callistus fades. He stood from his knelt position and pondered his conversation with the all mighty. Walking to the door, his head peeking out into the long hallway with candles guiding the way from each side of the hall, the two Swiss guards turn their heads and look upon the Holy Father. The Pope gives his commands to his young protectors. "Call out the guard. Find this Franciscan named Bernard from Prali. I want to see him before my throne." The youngest of the guards bows, and runs down the Vatican corridors. The Pope closes the door to his chambers, placing his robes upon his body. Behind him the stars begin to fade, the moon giving way to the sun, a new day is dawning.

As the sun rises upon Rome, a lone priest enters his quarters preparing for the day. Prayers and morning mass the thought of the day. The Franciscan looks over his daily itinerary until a loud knock disrupts him. "Please enter." the priest responding to the knock. A young brother enters the room, his voice nervous and excited. "Forgive me father Bernard. A Vatican guard is at the main gate requesting to see you." The Franciscan priest responds. "Did another Cardinal lose his cap again?" The priest walks out of his quarters and down the hall of the Franciscan mission, the young brother following close behind his hands shaking with nervousness, his mouth dry, teeth chattering. Looking out into the courtyard from an adjacent window he notices a Swiss guard on horseback, with another horse behind him, with no rider, the guard holding the reins. Father Bernard orders the gate to be opened with a calm but stern voice. Two brothers pull the large metal gate with their hands, the priest walking through with great confidence while the brothers groan, their sandals gripping the floor of the mission, doing all they can to make a good impression. Looking up towards the guard sitting upon his horse, the priest says. "What may we do for you here at Saint Blase?" "The holy father requests you to meet with him at once." The guard stammering his words while holding tight the reins of the horse. Father Bernard surprised with the request answered in kind. "Forgive me, but I don't think you are looking for me. You want Father Bernard of Prali?" The guard with his hard stare upon his face replies. "Yes of course, you are he?" "Yes I am he." With Bernard's confirmation of identity he orders the priest to take the other horse. Bernard lifts himself upon the horse and looks down towards the young monk standing at the gate. "I shall return shortly. Tell everyone to go on with their day and inform father Honorius that he is in charge till my return." The monk scurries off with his orders, the gates closing behind the Guard and the priest.

The journey to the Sistine chapel was a short twenty minute ride from the church. Rome was filled with churches and institutions. Every corner a church or convent was present. Bernard and his escort trotted between the large columns along Vatican square. The sound of the horse's hooves echoing through the square, the sun rising upwards, a fine day in Rome, while the white doves fly overhead and the people of Rome begin to wake and begin another day in the holiest city upon earth, a utopia, a heaven on earth. Arriving to the entry of the church, Bernard dismounts the horse, the guard doing the same, ordering the priest. "Follow me sir." Bernard did as ordered and followed the guard through the halls of the great church and headquarters of the Vicar of Christ. He had been to the Vatican on several occasions, but never to see the Pope. To see his holiness you had to have connections, connections Bernard did not possess. Two large golden doors opened before the priest and his escort. Etchings of angels and biblical scenes dominated the doorway. Inside the chapel paintings of past church leaders, from the first Pope Saint Peter to the present day Vicar, the art and statues that dominated the halls always fascinated Bernard. Walking down the red carpet the priest sees the Pope sitting on his throne, wearing a golden crown, and a purple scepter, the Holy Father wearing a basic white. Bernard wearing his priestly Franciscan garments kneels before the Pope, his head down to his chin. "Rise my Franciscan servant." With those words Bernard walked towards the Pope and kissed his holy ring. Callistus places his hand upon the priest and says a few words, the pope's power being felt upon him, or was it the Holy Spirit granting the power of prayer. Once the blessing finished, the priest stepped back and stood before the Pope. Bernard's heart racing with excitement, he wondered why he was called to such a grand experience. This monk from Prali has come a long way from polishing brass and cleaning monasteries.

The Pope looks towards Bernard and said to one of his guards standing beside him. "Bring the sword please." The guard exits the chapel, closing the door behind him. Bernard became nervous hearing the word sword. His mind running with thoughts of many scenarios and he became nervous and at the same time anxious. The guard returns with the sword upon a large purple pillow with gold trim. Placing the sword at the Pope's feet, Callistus waving towards the guard to assume his regular position, a command seen frequently by the guards, and all of those who work in Rome with the pope, it is the standard, no words, just actions. Bernard recognized the sword resting upon the pillow. It was the sword of Saint Peter. Bernard becoming uneasy and scared, Callistus turning his attention towards Bernard speaking with authority, "My friend, allow me to tell you a tale. Last night I slept comfortably in my bed, until a vision from God came to me. He showed me the victory of the dragon. He showed me everything. I am aware of your heroism. I have been instructed in this vision to give you a commission." Bernard looking worried with each word that withdrew from the lips of Callistus. "Father Bernard, you defeated the dragon and have been living in Rome for two years. In the past two years you have studied and became a priest. This is admirable coming from someone who use to milk cows in the little town of Prali. Now Bernard I must inform you of a new threat. The French town of Briancon has been eliminated from the face of the earth." Bernard's eye grew wide at the news of Briancon. The dragon returned?

Callistus continued with his devastating information. "Now the same threat that destroyed Briancon is now in Prali. For some reason the threat is using Prali, I don't know why." Bernard interrupted Caliistus. "Excuse me your holiness. Does this threat have a name?" The young priest curious and his question out of turn, and in the back of his mind the word commission worried him, he remembers his friend Leonardo who was granted a commission and ended up dead for it. Callistus only needed to give one name. "Simon Magnus, the first heretic." The priest's eyes grew wide, jaw dropping. "This is not the same Simon Magnus expelled by the apostles obviously.

That was so long ago." Callistus frowned. "The truth is that this Simon is thee Simon, it is he. He is a wizard of great power, and his deal with the devil made him almost invincible with extended life. I was briefed on old documents brought to me from the Vatican archives before I entered this room. Magnus has returned in the past and every time he returns the evil wretch is defeated. The only problem is he grows stronger with each reappearance. I am afraid he may now be unbeatable. The only weapon that can defeat him is the sword of the first Pope. You used this sword against the dragon, now I request you use it again. Use it on Simon Magnus. This time you must beat him for all times. He must never return. Simon must be sent home to hell. "Bernard could not believe his ears. "I'm sorry your holiness, I am just a priest now. The defeat of the dragon was just luck." Callistus grips his armrest and says. "No Bernard it was faith that won the day. You must return to Prali and stop this treacherous foe. If not he will convert the people to paganism, and great sin will erupt. All those of Prali will be converted and sent to hell. You must go and save the souls of your comrades. You have used the sword, you know the region. You are the only possible candidate. There is nobody with the knowledge and experience, you are the only one. Take the sword and be off with you. I will send with you ten knights of the Vatican. You will ride with my seal and my blessing. Return Prali to God and Magnus to hell."

Bernard steps back away from the Pope and places the sword of Saint Peter in hand, it feels light and steady. He bows to Callistus and says. "I shall do my utmost your holiness." The Pope stares into the priests eyes. "Yes for the sake of Prali and the entire world, we hope and we pray." Bernard steps back from the Pontiff. The guard turns to escort the Prali priest out of the building. Bernard thought of his past experience with the dragon, and the sword. He thought of the knight Leonardo, and wondered if this is how it was for the knight. To be given a grave mission from the Pope. Riding back to the church to gather his things under Vatican escort, he thought of one person he left behind in Prali. A good friend named Mary

Archer. He wonders if she stood to defend Prali against this Magnus character.

Prali, Italy. The local priest dead, a letter placed on the church door reads. "To the people of Prali, I hereby declare lord Simon Magnus head of the church in Prali. All business of Prali will be brought to his attention." People gathered to read the letter, Magnus hearing the clutter of people outside orders the church doors to be opened, his face gleaming with happiness. Decorus standing behind him wearing a black tunic fit for a Prince. "My people of Prali I am Simon. I have come far to serve you, and to give you the word of god. Your local priest has been transferred by orders of his holiness Pope Callistus II. My secretary Decorus will be assisting me in this great endeavor to make Prali a peaceful and tranquil town. Tonight a meeting will be held to explain the situation and to allow all to become acquainted." Decorus proceeded to pass out papers with information regarding the meeting. "Invite your families and friends. I pray the entire town will come and partake in this experience." Magnus grinning from ear to ear with his words of deceit among the people of Prali, Magnus looked upon them like sheep. The people of Prali taking the letters and sharing the information with all in town, word spread swiftly.

A knock on the door awoke Mary from her afternoon sleep. Opening the door she found her friend Annalisa. "Mary news in town, a new priest has come to Prali. He seems very nice and eager to communicate with the people. Unlike father DiNardi who was more of an administrator and not a man of the people, the new priest looks old but has vigor." Mary gave Annalisa a cold stare. "You woke me up with this news? I am planning on leaving. Why should I care if a new priest is in town?" Annalisa frowned and said. "There is a meeting tonight at the church. You should attend." Mary just turned and walked to her bedroom. "No Annalisa, I have no interest in such things. I will continue to get my beauty sleep." Mary's friend stammered with a response. "You have been a real bother since your mother passed Mary." The young English girl turns to her friend, and walks toward her in a confronting manner, slapping her friend in the face. "Don't you ever speak about my mother again!" Annalisa covering her red cheek with her hand, eyes watering, she moves away from Mary and leaves the house of her once good friend. Mary turned her back and walked to her bedroom.

The sun giving way to the moon and the stars, the air becoming crisp and chilling, a rare clear night for Prali in the first month of winter. The citizens of Prali filled the church of Saint Maximus. The church old and worn, its pillars ancient, filled with history of the town. Stain glass windows high above. In this day in age people could not read the bible for themselves, they relied on the church to teach them. The church was standing room only with the mayor being present and a new priest with a message, the town was excited and anxious. Mary riding her horse through town to clear her mind, wanting to find her friend and ask for forgiveness, she felt she was losing her mind. Since her mother's passing she has not been the same. Her friend nowhere to be seen, though the church caught her attention while she rides past, ever curious of the event taking place before her, so many people, the whole town was there. She has never seen so many people inside the church at one time; it brought great interest to her mind. Tying her horse across from the church, using a rope, placing it around a tree and kissing her steed's forehead, "Stay here, I shall return." Mary whispering in the horse's ear, she walks up to the steps of the church. Impossible to get into the church itself, doing her best to squeeze through the people, but to no avail, the church was overcrowded and deafening with gossip from the old women who were eager to see the new priest and filled with rumors. She decides not to give up, and forcefully she pushes people aside. Once the people realize who is pushing them, they allow her through. The entire town knew of Mary and her mother's death. In their sorrowful feelings for her they allowed her to pass through. Mary stood in the back of the church waiting to see who this new priest was.

Simon Magnus and his servant Decorus enter the church from behind the altar doorway. Everyone stands during the entry. Magnus steps up in front of the altar, taking center stage. Decorus standing by the corner, watching and listening, scanning the room filled with people. Magnus motions the people to remain seated; the crowd becomes hushed, waiting for Simon to speak. "Greetings to all the fine citizens of Prali, the Vatican sent me and my young ward to take over the duties from the last father who maintained this fine church. I am here to introduce myself to you. My name is Magnus; you may call me father Magnus. My young friend is named Decorus. He is a fine outstanding gentleman. If you have any questions you may come to him. He is at your service." Mary noticed Decorus. She smiles at his good looks and his fine clothes. He was too good to believe. She heard the girls behind her speak of him. They all wanted him for themselves. Mary decided to keep her attention to father Magnus.

Magnus continues to speak. Decorus notices Mary and smiles. He remembers the cave and his death from her arrow. Inside his mind he was still Skulk, to the rest of the world he is now Decorus. "I want to thank the mayor or Prali and all who attended tonight's meeting. Please come and join me for refreshments in the building behind the church. I will listen to you and be attentive to your needs." Magnus bowed to the people and not another word was said, not even a prayer for the people. Decorus followed from behind and said to Magnus. "I found her my lord. I found this Mary girl who ended my old life." Simon Magnus smiles an evil grin. "Good, good. Now everything is coming together." His laugh echoing through the halls, while the people of Prali shuffle out of the church one by one and into the streets, ranting and raving about this new event, the old women of the town creating new rumors among themselves. Everyone spoke of the new priest, and how concerned he seems for the people. Majority of the people went to take part eating refreshments and meeting the new priest. The mayor of Prali looked concern, and left the church. He didn't feel right about this priest. He wanted to go home and relax. All the girls of the town decided to stay and speak to Decorus. Mary standing in front of the church decided to come to the event. Not to speak to the new priest, but she felt a curious urge to attend. Her thoughts of observing got the best of her. She walked to the back and found herself in the middle of several of citizens wanting free food and conversing with each other. Mary standing in a corner watched the people. Magnus surrounded by the old women of Prali. Asking him questions in regards to the faith. He was eloquent in his words and sprinkled heresy with truth. His mission of disinformation has begun. Decorus surrounded by the most beautiful women in Prali. He never garnered this much attention in his life. He felt himself excited with all his prospects until Mary caught his eye. He located her standing in the corner. He politely excused himself from the hordes of beautiful women and made his way over to Mary.

"Hello my name is Decorus. Who might you be?" Kissing Mary's hand, a gentlemen's gesture, her face became red. "Thank you Decorus, my name is Mary Archer." "Well Mary it is a pleasure to meet you. I will be working here for some time. I have to admit I am taken by your beauty. Your accent, Is it English?" Mary blushed; for once she didn't mind being called beautiful. "Yes I am from Lancashire, England." Mary found herself spouting information freely, taken by his good looks and charm. "I live just outside of town, not too far." Decorus leaned on the wall, taking a comfortable position. "I see Mary, You have family I'm sure to help you around the home?" Mary silent for a moment, then answering his question with a calm innocent look upon her face, the candlelight within the room reflecting off her perfect complexion, her eyes looking into his, becoming mesmerized with curiosity and wonder for the man before her. "My mother just passed away. It is only me now. I plan on leaving this week and travel back to England." With sadness in his eyes he takes Mary's hand, caressing it gently. "Please Mary stay for just a week. I would really enjoy getting to know you better." His mesmerizing blue eyes, his blonde hair, it caught Mary off guard. She now is caught in his web of good looks and charm. "Decorus I figure you are not from around here. I don't find many men with your eye color and blonde hair." Decorus smiles, looking into Mary's eyes, "No I am actually from up north, the Baltic area." Mary blushes, smiling, looking into his eyes. "Tell me do you plan on joining the priesthood like your boss over there?" Decorus laughing slightly, "No the priesthood is not for me. I am just one who works for him." Mary made a sigh of relief towards his response. People began to crowd the conversation, the room becoming loud with talk and laughing. "Would you like to go outside where we can talk in peace?" Giving Mary the invitation, her heartbeat faster, "Yes I would enjoy that very much." Decorus places his hand into Mary's, guiding them outside to the church gardens, the moon shining upon their faces in the dark garden, Mary finding it difficult to keep her composure. She found herself falling for his charm. He guided her to a bench surrounded by flowers, a water fountain behind them. Only the moon gave them sight. Sitting together they continued the conversation.

"I have to admit I find Prali an odd place. The town is small compared to great places such as Rome." Mary asked with excitement. "You have truly been to Rome?" Decorus smiles, "Oh yes Rome is magnificent. I will have to take you there some day." Mary blushes, her heart racing. Her emotions never having the feeling she has now. "Tell me Mary are you seeing anyone? I mean do you have a man in your life?" Mary full of smiles answered. "No I have no one. I am a free bird." Decorus leans in towards Mary and says. "Please allow me to have the opportunity to catch this bird." Kissing Mary on the lips, feeling him upon her, she didn't push him away, she speaks within the kiss. "You have caught me." Her arms wrap around his muscular slender body, his fingers running through her hair. Their passion becomes ignited, the two moving together in motion, moaning softly, His hands gliding down her beautiful form. Their bodies becoming heated with passions never felt before. Suddenly the back door of the church opens. Two old ladies scurry out towards the garden. The two lovers move from each other. "Excuse me Decorus, I must be going." The young girl rises from the bench, Decorus not wanting her to leave, "May I see you again my beautiful bird?" she smiles, walking back to her horse. "Yes of course you can silly." Watching Archer walk across the garden and out of sight, Decorus smiles, he realizes his mission is almost complete. Nothing can stop him from ravaging Mary and taking her soul.

Outside of Rome a priest and ten Vatican knights leave the great western city of God, and head to the small village of Prali. Bernard thought of his adventure two years ago. He wanted to ride fast and arrive to Prali swiftly. The knights behind him followed. Bernard wanted no time wasted.

CHAPTER 5

The Rising Tide

Mary spent many wonderful moments with her new found love Decorus. She no longer pined for the life of her homeland. Her mind preoccupied with her one and only. Mary entertained him outside of her home on many occasions. Now Decorus rides out of Prali to complete a task ordered by his master. Decorus and Mary held each other, their hearts racing together as one. She looks up to him, gazing into his ocean blue eyes. "My love when you return will you bring back something special." Her love looks down, mesmerized by her pouty innocent lips, "When I return I shall ask for your hand in marriage." Mary smiles, their kiss imminent. They continue to hold each other, until the sun begins to dip behind the mountains. "I must go now Mary. I shall return to you, and when I do we will marry in Prali and I will take you and show you what it is like to lay with me." Mary's heart pounded. She wanted to be with him, still remaining strong, to save herself for marriage. One last embrace between lovers before Decorus mounted his horse and rode off into the sunset. She watches him till he was no longer visible, her heart captured, and weakened by love, or what she assumed was love. For Decorus it was revenge, to smite her. The young girl sighed looking in the direction of her love, the snow beginning to fall once more. The winters in Prali are legendary with cold winds and mountains of snow.

The church of Saint Maximus packed with parishioners, Magnus having the power of persuasion, using his magic to capture the minds of the people. He stands before the altar preaching to a full house of parishioners captured by his words of authority and charm, only the strong traditional Catholics scoffed at Magnus. The weak followers listened to Magnus like children, "My people of Prali! For too long we have followed the Church of Rome. They spin and weave their heresy. The Pope wears gold crowns, and builds large churches on the back of the poor. Is this Christianity? No I say not. I say to you people of Prali. Poverty and Austerity are the backbone of the true followers. I also say to you that personal study of scripture is needed. Why do you count on the words of man? These are just men, these priests and Popes. I came here to tell you there is a true way to follow God. Follow me and I will show you the way. The church sent me here to tell you this. To give you the freedom of thought, and to dispel Rome itself from the lives of holy men and women like yourselves. Come follow me and all will be given. You the people have authority, not the clergy." Majority of the people standing and cheering, their voices overpowering the large church, voices echoing through the ancient halls of this congregation, a chanting so deep in violence and hurt, a town fooled by one man, an evil that no townsfolk have ever set eyes upon. "Viva Magnus!" They shouted. The minority who felt insecure left silently. "My friends I say to you. If your mother, father, brother, sister, speaks well of Rome. Cut off their heads and send them for judgment. You will be blessed and taken to heaven on your day of entry. Do not stand and allow Rome to rule you. No longer, you are all free." The people continued to cheer. "Tonight is the night my friends. We take what is ours." Magus lifted his hands to the church ceiling, white beams shooting from his hands. Two angels above him appeared. The people in shock looked up towards the angels. The heavenly images looked down upon the people and said. "Follow Magnus, he has the power of heaven. What he says is truth. Go now and follow him."

The people of Prali fell to their knees, believing the angels above. What the people did not know is the angels are just a conjuring trick of a wizard. The angels faded, the white beams dissipating. Magnus looks down to the bowing people. "Now my friends, you have heard from heaven, now hear from your master. Go and kill anyone not believing in the true faith. Go now and cleanse Prali of its evil ways!"

The people stormed out of the church and filled the streets with hate and ignorance. Annalisa and Lacopo walked across from the church enjoying a comfortable winter's walk thought town. The couple stopped to witness the people gathering outside of the church. The people spoke anti Roman sentiment, and violence. Eight men who attended the meeting noticed Lacopo and Annalisa, "Hey you two! Come here I have a question for you." The lead man strong and bulky, a large man, Lacopo looking bewildered and uncomfortable, he realized something was amiss. The men intoxicated with the words of the wizard surround the young couple. The lead man asking, "Tell me my friends, is Rome the head of the faith?" Annalisa with no fear answered in kind. She assumed nothing would come from her answer since the men just left the church. She assumed the men must have heard a good homily. "My kind sir's this is an easy question. We all know there is only one true church. That is in Rome where the chair of Saint Peter resides." One of the men gripped the arm of the young girl, throwing her to the ground, her head hitting the cold ground. Lacopo launches his fist towards the hostile man, hitting him in the face. The eight men toss the young hero to the ground beating him brutally. The other people listening to Magnus run to watch the show. Annalisa in tears rises and runs for help, there is no one. Everyone is cheering the beating of her love. The red mark upon her forehead, blood trickling over her brow, evidence of the brutality of Prali, the girl running for her life not knowing if her love is dead or alive, her shock and disbelief of what has transpired. The men continue to attack Lacopo. The young man's bones heard breaking, the people laughing with every break. One of the men takes a piece of lumber in hand, bashing it against Lacopo's face. Lacopo lifeless and unrecognizable, the men beating him till he is no longer breathing, the attackers possessed with the words of evil. Three of the men lift the dead body from the ground and parade the victim around Prali town center. Laughing and cheering. "Down with Rome!" The body of Lacopo carried out to the local river, and tossed like an animal, his body floating down stream, Simon Magnus witnessing the event, and laughed. He no longer has to work to conquer the land, the people and the violence will prevail for him.

In her country home Mary rests in front of the fire, thinking of her new found love. Suddenly a knock at the door, the sound of a crying girl, Mary rushes to the door with great urgency. Opening the door she finds her friend Annalisa crying, her dress torn at the shoulder, her head bleeding profusely. Her cries are in hysterics; Mary guides her to the fire. "Annalisa what is wrong, please tell me." The distraught girl spent moments regaining her composure, finding courage to explain the attack. "Mary the men in the church, they attacked Lacopo and I. I'm not sure where my love is. The men attacked after listening to Magnus speak. The people shouted anti Roman propaganda." The young girl continues to cry, Mary stunned to hear the news listening to more of what her friend was saying. "I was running and noticed Magnus standing in the church doorway smiling. He wore a purple robe; his beard was unkempt and not tucked into his robes as usual. I swear I have never seen a man with a beard that long. It was down to his waist." Annalisa placing her head on a pillow, sobbing. Mary listened to her words about Magnus and realizing that her friend seemed out of her mind. To describe Magnus felt odd and thought her friend needed rest. She wondered if Decorus knew of the event.

Suddenly Mary wondered about the description of Magnus. Her jaw dropped, her body becoming uneasy and heated. Then she remembered. Her emotions getting the best of her, thinking of the Saint Bernard Pass, the hidden church, the dragon, and the man encased in ice. He wore a purple robe, long beard, the height being the same. Mary lifted Annalisa from the pillow, looking her in the eyes. Annalisa crying, her face red and exhausted. "Magnus, this man, he is no priest. He is something of a different nature. He is the one encased in ice, the dragons den." Annalisa shaking her head, "What are you saying Mary?" The young archer remembered. "Yes he is the one I found in the cavernous church of Saint Bernard." Mary nervous and scared, "I must do something Annalisa, this man is no priest, and what happened to father Denardi?" Questions swirled around Mary's head. Her discovery filled with shock and disbelief. "Magnus he must of killed the priest, and the rumor of Briancon is true. It all makes perfect sense." Annalisa could not understand her friend. "Mary the death of your mother, and your new man has made you ill. This cannot be." The hero stands, placing her hands over her mouth, then to her temples, in complete thought. "Oh no, Decorus works for Magnus. They are in league, and I fell for him. I have been betrayed." Mary pacing her living room thinking of what to do and how to get answers, her heart thumping in horror of the thoughts that ran through her mind. "Mary if what you say is true, there is nothing you can do about it. The people of Prali have taken arms against each other." Mary brainstorming, thinking of the events leading up to this rebellion against the Holy See, and the battle with the dragon in the sacred church on the pass, her mind filled with every conceivable thought and emotion. "Decorus said he is going to the town of Angrogna on a mission for Magnus. He left this evening; he is part of the upheaval." Mary became enraged with anger. Walking to her room, retrieving her black archer's uniform, equipping her sword, bow, and arrows, a dagger, and a crossbow upon her back. Facing her friend who is still laying her head on the pillow crying, "You stay in my home. Do not leave for anything. You will be safe here. If anyone knocks you must hide till I return." Annalisa seeing her friend could not believe her eyes, the friend she has never seen before, the girl warrior. Transformed into a fighter, a one man army, or one woman army, not the innocent girl from Lancashire that she knew running through the summer fields of Prali, or climbing the winter mountain tops of Italy, her friend was a different breed of woman. "Where are you going Mary?" Her friend mutters in anguish. "I am going to find Decorus and bring him to his knees." With those words the young warrior mounts her horse, riding to the town of Angrogna.

Angrogna another mountain town, another town on the brink of disaster, the citizens of this sleepy town ripe for the invasion of the evil ready to confront them and overtake them, unsuspecting women and children preparing for a night of relaxing slumber while the enemy is set for destruction and set forth the plans given to them by their master. Father Bernard and his ten Vatican warriors, looking over the town from a high mountainous elevation. "We will stay here for the night. I was here once before when I left Prali, and headed to Rome, I know a great Inn." The priest informing his men while the guards smile with a delightful grin and happy to finally rest for a night, the group traveled day and night, only stopping to water the horses, the urgency to reach Prali was the only thing on the minds of the small band of fighters accompanying the Franciscan. Bernard focused on his task and his worry for Prali, together with his longtime friend Mary Archer. One of the Vatican guards points to the north side of Angrogna, and says. "Look father, a fire seems to have erupted in the town." Bernard looks and agrees with his companion. Another guard speaks. "It is just a fire, a home as a matter of fact." A third guard notices another fire on the other side of town, pointing it out to the rest in the group. "Yes maybe a small fire. Look at the south and east side. They are now aflame." Bernard tightening his hands on the reins of his horse, realizing that these fires are connected. "Men there's something wrong, I think we have wandered into a war of some kind." A guard tries to extinguish the priest's thoughts. "No father impossible. No war here, where is the army?" Bernard with a fierce stare towards the guard says, "No my friend, a civil war of discontent and lies." The guards said not a word, Bernard moving his horse forward towards Angroga. The Vatican warriors following him down the small mountain pass.

Inside the town center of Angrogna, Decorus stands on top of a large statue overlooking the anarchy he caused. The horse statue placed recently by the town council, now his chair of command, leading his small band of heretics to destroy the town and convert the people of Angroga by the sword to the slavery of evil and wizardry. "This is the land of Magnus now!" he proclaimed, ordering his men to place the women of the town before him at his monument thrown. The men under his command, hired warriors from the east, old Saracens of the crusades and men who will sell their own children for a flask of ale, with the stench of their religion placed within their hearts and souls. The men dressed in tunics, and no visible armor, their faces hidden with a black facial covering, eager to rape and plunder the west, and the center of Christendom. Ten women placed before the fiend in charge of the expedition, all young girls between the ages of fourteen and twenty. Before the invasion of Angrogna, Decorus gave strict orders to bring all young girls before him for judgment. The girls crying in sorrow, their homes burnt down to the ground, Parents, siblings, husbands dead. Decorus wanted only the girls of the town saved. Every second another girl thrown into the town square for the judgment of Decorus. "Listen here girls. I will make this simple and easy for you. Two choices to consider and be sure you make the right decision, your lives are in my hands, now here are your options. One you renounce the faith of Roma, and you will be spared. You will then be married to one of my warriors and sent to the east. If you do not renounce the faith you will be killed right here at the town square as an example. Depending on your beauty, quality, and attractiveness, we will sell you into slavery. You will never see your homes again; you serve me and Magnus the great." Taking his sword from his side, pointing it towards one of the innocent girls in the square, a young Italian girl, age seventeen, a pure Italian beauty, her dress made from the finest tailors of Italy and the girl originating from an influential family, possibly a daughter of a political figure within the town. Decorus looking deep into her eyes, the evil warriors gathering around surrounding the girls, waiting to hear the decisions the girls will make, and hoping to be given a wife this very night, all the girls unblemished and innocent. The men battle hardened and fierce. "Tell me young girl. Do you choose death and slavery, or conversion and a strong man to care for you?" The young influential girl looks up towards her captor in defiance. "I choose to die, than to lay with your ugly men." Decorus turns his back on the girl, his anger building inside. Suddenly a swift turn towards the girl, a swing of the sword, the blade decapitating the young girl, her body falling to the ground, blood flowing. "Anyone else wants to try my patience?"

A calm voice from behind the eastern men answers the question of Decorus. "I would like to test your patience." The men of Decorus noticing the voice from behind and moving to the side exposing the one who speaks and surprised at what they see before them. Emerging from the men, Bernard and his fighters, with a look of defiance and readiness for a war, their armor shining from the town torches along the town square, and in this moment the town seemed to stop and silence fell around all within the square. Decorus shuttered seeing the priest, remembering two years before. He was a monk, the monk that killed the dragon, the one who assisted Mary Archer. The servant of the wizard looking towards Bernard and his men with a smug look upon his face, Bernard standing battle hardened. The smoke filled sky above them, the homes around the town square aflame. The work of the wizard's small army of assassins, a hired army of unconscious brutes handpicked by the wizard through his magic and influence, looking to conquer all who defy their faith and their homelands within the Middle East, working for Magnus to serve their own needs for world domination, thirsting for blood, victory, and all out revenge. Decorus gripped his blood stained sword. The blood flowing from the innocent girl, laying on the cobble stoned square. The sweat gliding from the evil servant's brow, down his cheek, his face marred with ash from the black smoke. Bernard looks toward the eastern men before him. "You men have a choice. To drop your weapons and surrender, or die trying to flee my sword of justice." The Vatican guards taking their swords from their sheaths, preparing for a fight, the easterners knowing the history of dominance the western crusaders had over them. "Girls may leave this square and go home. This town of Angrogna is about to be liberated from its brief occupation of evil heresy." The confidence of the priest amazed the servant of evil. How different this monk has become.

Decorus shrugged the monks challenge. He was afraid of the unpredictable monk, but kept his stance and defiance. "How dare you come to this place and challenge us priest. You have no authority here. We have conquered." The words of Decorus sparked his men to show their swords, and intimidate the priest and his companions. The young girls scattering from the town square, in fear of a battle. Decorus grew in anger his face showed aggravation. "How dare you scare my girls away from the square, you shall pay for this. The power of my god shall take care of you priest." Decorus drawing his sword and raising it towards the ash filled sky. The forty two eastern warriors under his command held tight their hilts. Bernard realized he and his men were surrounded. One of the Vatican guards stared the priest in the eye. "No worries father. We shall defend you in battle." Bernard smiled with a look of concentrated fear upon his face. "Yes my friend it is time for battle." Suddenly Decorus nodded towards his men, and the battle commenced. The Vatican guards defending Bernard, while the priest raises his sword to one of the eastern warriors racing to confront him in battle. The masked warrior with an unfamiliar weapon raised brought his first attack towards Bernard with a swing of his scimitar. Bernard turning to face the brute raised his short sword. The sound of clashing swords echoed through the cobble stoned square. The Vatican guards and the young priest now in a position of disadvantage, between the sounds of clashing Steele, Decorus could be heard giving orders and encouraging his men.

Bernard's sword making contact with the warrior of evil, his sword moving counter, while he places his body weight against his sword, the warrior much stronger pushes Bernard's sword away from him. Bernard stepping back, ducks towards the ground, swinging his sword towards the warriors knees. The warrior makes a counter move blocking the attack of the priest. He knew his sword was no match for this warrior. Clanging sounds and grunts heard around Bernard.

Falling between the Franciscan and his enemy, a Vatican guard who was fatally hit by enemy sword, a strike to the chest, blood flowing upon the cobble stone. Bernard leaps over the dead body of his comrade and tackles his enemy. Reaching for his dagger attached behind his back, striking his enemy in the heart. The warrior drops his sword, blood spitting from his mouth. The priest now lying upon his dead enemy turns his head to look at his men. Only four of his men left and twenty of the eastern horde remain. Taking his sword in hand, the priest whispers. "Saint Peter I call on you to guide me in the battle against the snare of darkness." Suddenly and sensation from the sword runs through Bernard's body. Rising from his position upon his dead enemy, he looks and finds his men battling for their lives. Decorus joins his men in battle against the Vatican warriors. Bernard rushing into the fight, while he watches two more of his men fatally hit the ground, the priest entering the battle, his sword swinging with wild passion striking one of the men of Magnus in the chest. Two more warriors approach Bernard. The priest turns to the warrior towards his right side, their swords connecting with a fierce clang. The second warrior rushes behind Bernard with blind fury while the young Franciscan launches his right leg hitting the warrior in the stomach, his balance upheld by the sword upon the other warrior. The warrior falls back with the impact of Bernard's boot. The priest facing the warrior with sword before him and launches his fist toward the enemy. Making contact, the warrior stunned in disbelief over such an attack by a holy man. Bernard taking his sword, severing the head of the enemy, turning to face more attacks from the Far East fighters, but to his dismay disappointment and sorrow, realizing all of his men are dead, the enemy now faces him with five men and Decorus. The smoke growing intense while the city continues to burn, people in the town occupied with saving their homes and families. Bernard realizes there are more of the enemy running the streets killing and burning Angrogna. In time the whole army would come down upon him. If he could kill the five men and Decorus, he would stand a fighting chance to run and find help.

Decorus laughs while his men stand behind him, his hands upon his waist, "Ok monk, or should I say priest now. This insurrection is over, time to give up." Bernard wondered how this enemy knew of his past as a monk. Did he meet this man before? Bernard thought of all the people he had come across in the last few years. Nothing came to his mind of ever meeting a man with blonde hair and blue eyes. Not recently anyways. Suddenly a whizzing sound past the ear of Bernard, one of the eastern warriors falls to the ground, and then another, Bernard confused, Decorus in a panic. The priest notices a red feathered arrow sticking out of the warrior's chest. A familiar voice is heard above a burning roof top. "Oi Bernie! Let's finish this mess shall we!" The young priest dared not turn his head in fear of his enemy charging him. He knew the voice; a smile came upon his face. It was his old friend, Mary Archer. Suddenly another arrow strikes the enemy. Bernard charges towards Decorus, while the last man of the eastern warriors falls to the ground with a crash to the cobble stone square. Decorus and Bernard running towards each other, swords in the air, the whizzing sound of arrows being heard, Mary was attacking Decorus. The swords clash, Bernard kicking his foot behind the leg of Decorus, using his weight to push him over onto the ground, Decorus dodging arrows, his sword connecting with Bernard's, the two men in a struggle for survival, fighting for control of the town and their ideals, the follower of the wizard knowing he must win or his master would scold him with fierce anger. Before he knew it, he was on the ground, the sword of the Franciscan priest in his face, the sound of arrows in flight ceasing. "Now my friend do you plan on surrendering now?" Bernard now speaking with great confidence, Decorus spits upon the ground. "I shall never give up. My master is great and powerful. You are a dead man. You just don't know it yet. My warriors are throughout the city killing the innocent people of this ravaged town, you cannot stop it." Suddenly behind Bernard Mary is heard. She looks down towards deplorable Decorus. "How could you have done this Decorus. I thought you were one of the good guys." Decorus looks away from Mary and says. "It's not I who am evil, but this priest." Mary laughs and looks at Bernard, "Oh a priest? Congratulations on the promotion Bernard." The priest smiles and responds. "Thank you."

Behind Mary and Bernard charging armor his heard, more of the warriors under the command of Decorus rushing to defeat the heroes, Mary turns and launches another volley of arrows towards the men. Bernard allowing his guard to be dropped turns to face the new challenge, his body exhausted from the previous battle and his men dead, with only the girl to assist him. Decorus realizes this is the perfect time to flee. Rising from the ground, he runs out of the city of Angrogna, his feet tripping over the cobblestones, his heart racing in fear. You can change his name from Skulk to Decorus, but deep down inside he was still the wretched dragon slave. Bernard meeting the swords of the fierce warriors, swinging his sword and hitting one of the warriors in the chest without a thought, his actions taken in pure defensive measures, the man falling to the ground in agony, blood rushing from his body like a geyser, body shaking in convulsions, his hands clutching his heart knowing he is gone from terra firma. Taking another dagger from his back he throws the dagger, hitting the other warrior in the neck. Blood sprouts from his neck, while he falls to the ground, holding his neck in pain, a slow death. Mary doing what she does best, striking in the hearts of her enemy with her arrows, the warriors all falling to the ground, blood gushing and flowing from their bodies like a river of death and fear, the battle becomes silent as the enemy falls to nothingness. "I guess if they were smart they would have been wearing chain mail. Those eastern blokes never wear armor." Bernard chuckles and says. "You mean macula?" Mary smiles and responds. "Yeah if that is how a man with education says it." Mary embracing Bernard, "It has been two years my friend. How are you? I guess you are no longer a monk." Bernard wraps his arms around his friend, then releasing his hold, in answer to her questions. "True I am a priest now, a Franciscan priest. I was doing my duty till the Pope requested to see me." Mary laughed. "You mean ordered you." Bernard's face grew red. "Yes he ordered. He had a dream about the dragon slaying. In short he ordered me back to Prali and the Turin province. He spoke of a great enemy of the church named Simon Magnus." Mary balked at his words. "Enemy, he is more than that my friend. He is the devil himself. My friend is hiding in my home for fear of her life. This man Magnus came into town not long ago and declared that the church sent him. The people believed and followed him, but not all."

Bernard placed his sword in his sheath and continued speaking to Mary. "That is not all. The Vatican has reports that he may have destroyed the town of Briancon. Have you heard news?" Mary placing her hand on her chin. "Things are so confusing to me now after all that has happened. If what you say is true, then we must stop this mad man." Bernard responds back relaxing his stance. "You mean I, this mad man is no regular man, and he is a wizard. He learned his skills from the old traditions of wizardry, before the God of this time. He wants to bring back paganism by using heresy. He is a wizard of great power. Mary shook her head. "If he uses magic then it is confirmed he is from evil. Only magic comes from evil. Using magic will open the gates of hell upon the earth." Bernard shaking his head in agreement, "This is why Prali is now in sin and despair. If this thought of magic being good reaches the world. All can be lost. Satan will reign once more. Though he reigns now, with magic he can control the minds of people. We cannot allow Magnus to bring back creatures of the past like dragons, elves, demons." Mary looks around to see the smoke and fire around them. "Bernard it is not you who will fight Magnus, we both will. You will need my help. I think I did a good job covering you tonight." Bernard sighs, "I guess I have no choice Mary. Yes together again." Mary smiles, "I would not have it any other way." Mary pausing then continuing, "Now what shall we do about Angrogna?"

Bernard worked the streets and homes of Angrogna, while Mary jumped from rooftop to rooftop firing her arrows at unsuspecting enemies. The fire spreading, Bernard noticing town members walking and running in confusion, he grabs one of the men by the collar. "What are you doing man?" The citizen of Angrogna stares into the eyes of the man. "Listen I don't care how shocked you are. Gather your people and find buckets. Fill them with water and help get this inferno under control." The man continued to stare out into the burning buildings. Bernard raises his fist and slaps the man with the palm of his hand. The man suddenly stands at attention. Bernard repeats his instructions once more. "Yes father I shall do as you wish." The man scurrying off to complete the task given to him by father Bernard, while word through the city spread that Decorus escaped from harm. Rumor spread that he ran from a priest and a girl, the talk spreading faster than the fire. Many of the eastern warriors witnessed the evil servant running back towards Prali. One thing eastern warriors did not respect was cowardice. Many who heard of this truth left for the east, never to return to Italy again. They knew their skills would be better served in the crusades against the Christians. Bernard came across little resistance. He found himself organizing groups of men to extinguish the fires throughout the city, the women also lending a hand. Word reached the past the border of Angrogna of a priest who saved the city from the invaders. The people of the city regained their confidence and their sense of community, helping one another in the struggle to save the city from fire. The girls who scattered from the town center, returned to clean the blood from the cobblestone, and to carry the dead girl at the hands of Decorus back home.

Mary running from rooftop to rooftop, her heart racing, her feet balancing on the edge of the buildings, the streets of Angrogna below her, she notices the eastern warriors running from the city. She fires her arrows jumping from one roof to another. The arrows launching and hitting the runaway warriors from behind, she showed no mercy. In her mind she thought of the deception of her love. She was used and regretted opening her heart. She became hardened in her heart with every launch of the arrows. She wanted to kill Decorus, and the men who followed him. Every man she killed, she wanted it to be the one who used her. One by one the warriors fell to the girls arrows, running faster and faster. The arrows launching at lightning speed, no visible warrior could escape the wrath of Mary Archer.

Suddenly she ran out of rooftop almost falling off the last building of the town. Stopping her feet cold on the edge of town, behind her smoldering buildings, in front of her warriors escaping for their lives not looking back, running home to the desolate east where only dogs and dirt are content. To her surprise she won the day, along with Bernard. She turned to head back to the square where she first found her friend. There she found him, tending to those in need. She approaches him with caution, wanting not to distract him. She leaned against a building and watched his magic, the magic of a true heart, a Franciscan who wanted to change the world for the better. His magic was not of wizardry of witchcraft. It was the magic of love for fellow man, the greatest power on earth. She watched while he completed his task of humanitarian and priest. Slowly she slides her body down the building wall, and sat on the ground waiting. Her eyes growing tired from the journey originating in Prali, and the evenings battle.

"Wake up Mary." Bernard's voice ringing out with the glare of the morning sun upon her face, "We must travel to Prali, the sun is shining and we must take advantage of this weather break before it starts to snow, it will get cold in the evening and I am not too prepared for a snowfall" Mary rubbing her eyes, and rising from the ground. "Sorry I must have fallen asleep. I have a horse just yonder. Allow me to fetch the beast. I will meet you back here at the square." Mary sleepily stumbles to the north side of town to retrieve her steed, the priest relocating his horse, and in charity giving the other horses belonging to his Vatican guards to a local farmer. The Franciscan and the archer met one last time in the center square of the town. "Well Mary looks like we have another long day ahead of us. We must make it to Prali by tonight." Mary yawned. "Yes no problem. I made it to Angrogna in no time, not a bad ride at all. We may make it by this afternoon. On the other hand Bernard you need rest." Bernard gripping tight the reins of his horse, "No time for sleep, sleep is for the dead." The girl smiles and responds. "Granted I swear I was dead asleep last night." Bernard shaking his head listening to the girl's words, urging his horse to travel north to Prali and investigate the evil deeds of one wizard, he hoped to return to Rome soon and inform the powers to be his findings in the region. Mary close behind, the two friends leaving the town of Angrogna, and heading to Simon Magnus in Prali.

Decorus angry at his defeat, riding a black horse he stolen from a local stable, "That damn girl, and her religious friend. They won again, but for the last time. Once they meet Magnus, they will fall to his power." He spent no time stopping to water the horse he continued with haste. He knew Mary and Bernard would be fast behind, and heading towards Prali. It is only a matter of time till the confrontation takes place. Suddenly a thought came to the evil servants head. He remembered a troll in an adjacent forest to Prali. His evil mind begins to scheme, riding towards the forest of the last troll upon the earth. The woods vast, and only used by local hunters and thieves during the daylight hours. In the night the troll scoured for food, and to survive in the world of man. Deep in the forest a hidden cave, only known by scoundrels such like Decorus, the entrance covered in moss, large rocks blocking the entry. Trolls are huge creatures weighing over five hundred pounds, and over ten feet in height. Their body built like hard boulders, and muscles larger than the average man. The troll would move rocks into position before the sunrise covering the entrance to the cave. During the day he slept and hid from man. He feared man, knowing he is the last of his kind. This creature is the type Simon Magnus promised to bring back to the world after his rule is complete. To bring back the old realm of Elves, Dwarves, Trolls. It was the first step in reinstituting pagan rule once more, the death of man, and the creatures of old reborn. He also wondered why the furies didn't come to his aid while he battled the priest and the archer. Magnus promised their protection. If these creatures were not capable of helping him what good can they be.

Decorus doing his best to push the rocks from the entry, to no avail, the Troll hearing the grunts and groans of a desperate man, on the other side of his rock barrier, curiosity gets the better of the lumbering Troll, rising from his slumber he walks over to the blocked entry. The groans are louder, he realizes now that a human is trying to enter his domain. The troll sits and waits for the man to enter is cave. On the other side of the rocks Decorus pulls and prods his way, not knowing what waits for him on the other side of the rock wall. He wished his master gave him magic powers to move the large boulders. Two hours later he felt the rock move slightly, a gap just enough for him to slide between the rocks. He moves between the humongous rocks, hoping they don't fall back into place and crushing his delicate human form. Heavy breathing and sweat dripping from his face, he makes it to the other side and makes it within the cave. To his amazement the troll sits watching him with only a loin cloth upon his body, his chin resting on his large hand. "So human you come into my home and without an invitation." Decorus is shocked, not prepared for such a sight. "Yes sir I came to see you. My master has knowledge of the forgotten world. He wishes to bring it back to life." The troll laughs while responding. "Your master wants to bring back the old ways? He is lost. Look at this world. These humans are decease. They kill each other for sport. They are the worst of all created creatures. They have taken control and an unmovable foothold on the world. My time is done. I wish only to die in this cave, and be forgotten." Decorus amused towards the trolls defeated attitude. "Look troll I have something for you, a chance to kill humans, and to possibly die a hero's death." The troll entertained by the words he hears, finding his human trespasser a laugh. "Humans I can kill. Why do you think these woods have a bad name? It is because of me. I have become a legend to the human race. Nobody comes here at night for fear of the great legend. Many humans I have killed in these woods. Just to keep the legend alive. If humans feel these woods safe, then they will find me and vanquish me." Decorus smiles and responds. "First you say you want to die, then you say you kill people to keep them from killing you. Make up your mind troll." The troll pondered the words of the trespasser and says. "I guess you have a point, and what may I ask do you suggest."

Decorus realizing he may get his wish continues to speak to the troll, giving him an offer. "My dear troll friend, coming this way is a fierce monk and a girl. They want to kill all of you creatures that I hold dear. They want to end the old realm completely. They come this way to do so. In the distance there is a bridge that connects to the road heading towards the town of Prali. They will take this road, and need to cross the bridge. My master and I ask you to stop them at this bridge location. The male is a monk, a Christian monk. He belongs to the same faith that destroyed the world, and made it their own. This is a chance for redemption." The troll with a grimace and a look of deep thought. Decorus standing and waiting for the trolls reply. "These two humans, they want to finish off the old realm you say?" "Yes of course they are Christian. Anything of the old realm is evil, you know this already, and you know history. How old are you a thousand years old?" The troll looks up to the cave ceiling, in his mind counting, then looks down towards Decorus. "No I am exactly one thousand and ten . . . . Wait . . . . one thousand and eleven." Decorus interjects. "Will you do it for the realm and my master?" The troll looks down at the human, his hands clinched. "I will not do it for your master or for the realm. I will do it for me and my old friends, the ones who died at the hands of these Christians. I will seek vengeance and kill this meek monk. No monk is fierce. I will end this human's life and send him to the God he worships so dearly." Decorus smirks with the look of evil upon his face.

CHAPTER 6

The Toll Bridge and the Servant

The day falls into night. Light snow falls lightly upon the cold terra firma. Two lone riders in the distance coming closer to the bridge of Prali, the nostrils of the steeds releasing steam., the hooves clomping upon the cold snowy earth, one of the riders a monk, the other a girl. Underneath the bridge a dark figure hides waiting to wreak havoc upon the riders, the figure is Decorus the follower of Magnus, and accompanying him is the troll of the old earthly realm. "They are coming good troll." Decorus speaks with excitement in his voice. The troll moves his head from under the bridge just slightly to observe his victims. The river steep and treacherous, only by the bridge can someone enter Prali from this location. The troll looks at Decorus with eyes of death and a thirst for human blood, no mercy for the oncoming riders. "I will avenge all that is dear to me. I have no reason to live on this new earth. I will kill these riders, and join your master in destroying the race of man. I will remerge, and be victorious, honoring my ancestors. How I have grown lonely all these years, hiding in the forest for all this time. Before the Roman Empire I hid. Now I make myself known in sight of the world. I have returned to seek vengeance, and now is my time." Decorus smiled thinking of this plan perfect in every way. He thought he would never talk the troll into fighting.

It seems to Decorus that the troll wants to end it all. No matter the consequences. The troll moves from his position underneath the bridge. Climbing the steep grade, and placing his humongous form before the bridge. His bulky arms, his body of pure muscle standing in the way of Bernard, Mary, and Prali, the troll cracking his knuckles in preparation for the conflict with his new found enemy.

The priest and archer riding swiftly notice a large form upon the bridge. Bernard stops his horse, Mary following his lead. "What do you make of that Mary?" The monk queries, the girl looking towards her friend with a slight look of concern. "I have no idea. If he came from Prali, than we have trouble." "Whatever do you mean?" Bernard continuing to speak with a raised brow, the girl connecting the dots, "Think about it Bernie, Magnus in control of Prali, and spreading his hate. You think a hunk of a figure like that can be good in any way?" Bernard looks around him, and then rides forward towards the bridge, the snow falling upon his priestly robe. "Mary, now that you mention it. You have to be right. Never have I heard or seen such a huge mass of a man. Let's investigate this and make our discovery, this man may have answers to our curiosity." The two friends continue to ride. Closer and closer they come to the lone figure of muscle upon the bridge. Suddenly the huge figure comes into full view. Mary stops her horse, and Bernard follows suit. "Ok Bernie. You honestly think that ugly thing is a good thing?" The two friends seeing it is not a man at all, but a creature of some kind. "I would have to assume that this thing on the bridge is not a good thing. Like I say though, we must not judge a book by its cover. Maybe he was thrown out of Prali for being ugly." Mary gives Bernard a queer look. "Ok Bernie so you are telling me that mass of ugliness is a human?" The priest with a slight look of fear and curiosity for the troll responds to Mary. "I think we should not judge until we speak to this person, or thing." The girl responds in a loud tone. "Judge this thing? I can tell you he is here for harm." Bernard speaking with a saintly tone counters his friend. "Ah my young lady, we must not judge, lest we be judged." Mary growing a bit aggravated speaks. "I am not judging. Look at that thing. You are telling me he is normal? You think he is a safe bet? I doubt it." Bernard gives Mary a look of challenge. "Well young girl let's ride and speak to the poor unfortunate thing." The English girl tightens the reins and kicks her horse lightly. "Very well father Bernard, oh holy man of the world." The priest not appreciating her sarcasm rides adjacent to her, coming ever closer to the troll upon the bridge.

Mary and Bernard now face to face with the troll, only twenty feet separated them from the hideous creature of doom. Mary looking at the huge mass of muscle with awe, her jaw dropping, eyes rising, looks up towards the beast from his toes to his head. Bernard doing his best to look strong and confident, words escaping his lips, introducing himself to the troll and praying in his heart that this will not end in bloodshed and violence, the troll with his piercing eyes and mammoth build looking at these two weak humans and thoughts of crushing them running through his mind. "Good day fine sir." The troll huffs towards the priest and answers. "Good? Good you say? What may I ask is so good about today? It is cold and the snow gets worse." Bernard smiles towards the troll blocking his path to Prali. He feels secure in his conversation with the troll; he thought speaking was a good thing. The creature speaks and is non-threatening. "Yes my good friend. It is winter and Prali is a place of snow fall every winter. Are you not from around here dear sir." The troll laughs. "Yes I am from around here. I was here before you were born. I was here before the Romans. I was here before your Christ. I was here before the dawn of man." His left hand clinched and lightly punching the palm of his right hand. Bernard curious of what the troll speaks continues his dialogue. "Well good sir I am not one to know of such things. I am only here to pass, and ride into Prali. The town just beyond your shoulders there," Bernard lifting his head to peer over the trolls shoulder. "Sorry monk but before you can pass the bridge you must pay a bridge toll to me." Mary hearing the trolls words laughs and speaks. "You are kidding me? This is like the story my Mother would tell me before bed." The troll looks towards the innocent looking girl with the pearl white skin, and pouty red lips. "I'm sorry young thing. I am not sure of what story you speak of." Mary doing her best to control her chuckles, "You know the story, the troll and the toll bridge." The troll growing angry responds. "Well girl I have to tell you that I am a troll, and if you don't have the money you will not pass." The priest begins rustling within his habit searching for coin and finally pulling coins from his robe, and presenting them to the troll, the money resting in his palm making it visible to the troll, "Is this enough to pass toll troll?" The two friends doing their best trying not to snicker knowing the old tale of the troll and the bridge, even the archer girl found it odd that the troll did not know of the story. The troll responds, "No that is not enough. It will cost you one-thousand coins to pass." Mary tightening her grip on the reins of her horse saying. "Nobody can afford such a toll. You are wild. Has anyone ever paid this toll? Last time I checked this bridge was a free bridge. Is your master Magnus, has he told you to control this bridge?" The troll responds to the young archer with slight anger in his voice. "I know no Magnus. This is now my bridge. I serve no master." The troll raising his fist in the air, his demeanor commanding and resolute with only one thing on his mind, to kill the little rats before his eyes and return to his cave with feelings of revenge subsided.

Bernard moves his hand to the hilt of his sword. The sword of Saint Peter, used by many in the past including Saint Bernard and Peter himself to defend Christendom from the gates of hell and the underworld of evil demons, the same sword used to protect the Lord in the garden of Gethsemane. Bernard acquired the sword while on his mission to kill the dragon two years ago. The sword slayed the dragon, and also Simon Magnus long before Bernard and Mary walked the earth. "Sir if you call yourself a troll I will not argue your points. We must pass, and have not the money you require. Is there any way we may help you or make up for the money." The troll laughs and responds to Bernard. "Yes if you fight each other to the death. The victor may pass." The priest becoming irritated with the troll says. "This will not happen. We would like to cross the bridge please." Bernard speaking with calm in his voice, the troll flexing his muscles responding to the diplomatic priest from Rome who seems arrogant in the eyes of the creature from the old world of magic and might. "Sorry monk. It looks like we have a conflict. No more words, time to face your judgment." Bernard holding tight to his sword makes no hasty moves. He wants to avoid violence. Mary on the other hand lifts her bow from around her shoulder, and takes one of her arrows in her left hand. The troll see's the archers actions and prepares for the conflict he has been waiting for. "Sorry monk and his little female friend. I will not allow you to pass, over my dead body." His laugh growing sinister, face growing in anger, mentally the troll psyching himself up for battle and the victory to soon be at hand, his body feeling heated as the fight is inevitable, only one answer for him, victory and revenge. Mary and Bernard turn their heads to one another. They give each other the look of desperation and of no choice. They realize they must face the troll. The young archer raising her bow and arrow towards the troll states, "Dear sir we will pass now and you will move aside. Failure to do so will cause us to wreak havoc upon you. We are on mission by orders of his holiness the Pope." The troll laughs and smiles with glee. "Dear girl. I know of no such person that you mention. I do not abide by humans. You may not pass."

Suddenly behind the troll on the other side of the bridge, Decorus stands, his sword in hand. "Kill those Christian bastards!" Bernard looking towards the other side of the bridge notices Decorus, and pulls his sword from his sheath. Mary noticing Decorus feels her anger grow and the feeling of betrayal overcome her thoughts. Without hesitation Mary launches the arrow towards the troll, the creature noticing Decorus turns toward the evil villain who talked his way into fighting the Christians, his back turned from Mary and Bernard. Mary's arrow flying through the air hits the troll in the left shoulder. Blood flows from the penetrating arrow, the wound grows with flowing blood. The troll turns to face his foes. With a laugh and a smile he launches his body towards the young girl, the huge mass of muscle charging the archer from Lancashire, the sound of the ground shaking below the feet of the two friends, the troll's muscles flexing with tremendous power, a battle commencing, a fight to the death. Noticing the troll's actions Mary jumps from her horse, and places another arrow in her bow, another launch, another arrow. In midair the troll catches the arrow in hand, crushing it with his force. Mary's horse runs off into an adjacent meadow. The sound of the beginning battle scaring the horse. Bernard rushes toward the troll with his mighty steed. His sword in hand, and pointed forward. Like a general calling the alarm to charge the enemy. The troll is almost upon Mary. Nothing she can do but launch herself towards the troll, aiming her slender body towards the ground. The troll flying above her while she launches and falls to the ground. Bernard simultaneously hits the troll with his horse, while the troll and the horse colliding with a mighty bone crushing sound from behind Mary. The young archer turns to face the carnage. Bernard on the ground, his sword some distance from the collision, the horse on the ground, not moving. The troll staggering to his feet his body yearning for air while he gasps, the attack from the priest surprised the over confident creature. Mary raising herself from the ground launches another volley of three arrows towards the troll. All three a direct hit to the neck. Bernard slowly rises and searches for his sword. He finds it in the tall grass next to the roadside. The troll standing with four arrows protruding from his humongous body turns to Mary and charges once more. Mary firing her arrows without mercy, one, two, three, four, arrows hitting the troll, blood flowing from the large monster, the archer realizing one hit from the troll will kill her. She runs towards the bridge away from the troll. Decorus now standing in the middle of the bridge watching the battle between the three laughs and finds the situation entertaining, he forgets himself and all that he did to Mary in Prali.

Bernard taking his sword in hand rushes to help his friend in the conflict. Mary stops shy of the bridge. Not wanting to come between the troll and Decorus. She knew fighting both would be folly. The evil henchmen with his arrogant smile stands with his arms folded, entertained by the battle. Mary turns to face the rushing troll, his large body crushing the ground under him, the thumping sound of his charge heard loudly. The troll launches once more, his large clinched fist leading the way. Once again the swiftness of the young archer moves from her foe with a roll and tuck to the ground, the troll landing on the bridge with a crash taking out a large section of the wooden bridge. Pieces of lumber falling one hundred feet below, "Stop playing!" Decorus shouts towards the troll. Bernard now running behind the troll catches up and strikes the troll with his sword, before the troll can recover from his collision with the bridge, the sword slicing through the troll's armored skin. The creature rising, doing his best to disregard the searing pain coursing through his body turns to face the monk who struck him with the sword. Bernard standing before the troll, blood sliding down the blade and dripping onto the Franciscans hands, while he holds the sword upright, his heart pounding with excitement and uncertainty, his mind focused on the task at hand not knowing if he and his friend will make it past this challenge. "Have you had enough troll?" Bernard questions loudly. The troll in pain laughs. "No priest I have only just begun!" Suddenly more pain from behind the troll. Four more arrows enter his body. The troll confused. Who to attack? The monk with sword, or the girl with her arrows, his mind spinning with thoughts of his next move not sure who to fight, he was perplexed? Thought being the troll's weakness since trolls always attacked in groups of four or more. While in thought four more arrows hit him from behind. He turns towards Mary, continuing his attack on her. Running once more towards the archer's position, the priest following the troll doing his best to hit the creature with his sword, the shaking ground making his attack difficult even for a creature as large as the troll, it felt like a quake under his feet. Mary standing adjacent the bridge, the enemy charges with all the power of a troll, her mind and body preparing to make a swift decision and then suddenly she darts towards the edge of the cliff. Down below one hundred feet is the river. The troll stops in his tracks and turns towards Bernard, who is close behind the troll. The priest seeing his foes turn towards him cannot react swiftly. Stopping in his tracks he stumbles and falls forward, the troll Grabbing Bernard and throwing him towards the bridge. The priest flying through the sky, unaware of his direction, and landing point, hitting the large planks upon the bridge loses consciousness.

Mary launching more arrows towards the menacing enemy, all a direct hit as blood spurts from the enemy. The troll covered in his own seeping blood. Mary feeling the edge of the cliff behind her heels steadies herself for another launch of the troll. Now weakened from arrow penetrations, the troll charges Mary once more. Stumbling on his way towards her, he falls hoping to land and crush the girl. Mary once again moves to the side. The troll not realizing his surroundings finds himself falling from the cliff. He falls past Mary and down the edge of the cliff, meeting his doom landing upon the sharp rocks below the flowing river. His loud screams being heard until silence, his bloody body mixing with the snow, and water from the river's edge, the last of his kind wiped from the earth. Decorus walks over to Bernard, looking down upon the Franciscan priest. Nothing can stop him from killing Bernard now. Finally victory will be his. "Poor little monk, time to die." His voice of evil informing the unconscious hero of his fate, pulling out his sword directing the point towards the helpless hero, evil making its mark upon his enemy and revenge for his first death in the mountain cave of Saint Bernard's Pass, he relished in the soon to be victory. Suddenly Decorus remembers the sword, the sword of Saint Peter. His eyes scan the area, no sword to be found. First he will kill Bernard then find the sword, lifting his weapon over his head, both hands grasping the hilt." You shall die! This is for killing me in the dragon's lair!" With the words of Decorus, Bernard finally opens his eyes. His first image is of Decorus and the raised sword. Decorus tightens his grip upon the hilt. His final move is to swing down his weapon to kill Bernard. A familiar pain rushing through his body, looking down towards the ground seeing an arrow and blood, Mary striking his chest, his grip loosens upon his sword. Another arrow enters his body, going through his black deceitful heart. His grip no longer exists while his sword lands on the ground behind him. His eyes glance to see Mary standing in the adjacent meadow. Her bow and arrow rising towards him once more, the light wind slowing through her delicate brown hair, the look of victory upon her face, the girls smirk gave Decorus the answer. He was already dead. His body falls backwards upon the hard deck of the bridge.

Mary runs to help her friend. "Are you ok Bernie?" She questions with exhausted breath. Bernard lifting himself up from the hard lumbered bridge responds. 'Yes thank you Mary. You are really a God send." Dusting the dirt from his habit, they both turn to see the dying Decorus, his body limp, his eyes closed, finally one last breath of life. Slowly the young attractive Decorus begins to change. His skin becomes old and wrinkled, his hair falling from his head, body mass changing to a slender scrawny creature. "Skulk?" Bernard queries, the girl not saying a word, her mouth drops to the ground. Her embarrassment of the situation grows within her mind. Lucky for her nobody is aware of her love for Decorus, who was actually Skulk. Her demeanor showed disgust, she wanting to cry, holding back her tears. She felt dirty, and used. "Can you believe this is actually Skulk?" Bernard in disbelief while the girl takes the limp worthless dead body of the wretched thing and throws the weak body of the creature over the bridge, and falling down below to rest with the dead troll. Looking towards Bernard while she wipes her hands upon her clothes feeling the dirt upon her hands, "No Bernard I cannot believe that was Skulk. If it was then he is no more, and we shall never speak of that creature. He is over with." She turns away from her friend and walks to find her horse in the meadow. Bernard surprised at the tone of his friend, she seemed to shutter finding out Decorus was actually the demented creature from the dragons den. Bernard thought it must bother her to kill a foe twice. He remembered his horse running over to see if his mount needed his attention, the horse stood strong, ready to continue on the journey to Prali.

In the town of Prali the mood somber and reserved, the people were taken over by one powerful wizard, falling into place and accepting Magnus, after he supplied them with all their needs of food clothes, and weapons, the wizard buying their allegiance. Magnus continues to supply the people with bread and wine; he looked like a missionary for a people with no monetary means since he cleaned out the coffers of all the citizens. He tells the people that they have no need for money, that he will supply them with every need. With his powers he creates the food supply. The food laced with a sedative to calm the people, making them more agreeable. The doctors left Prali only the day before. No longer are the physicians needed. Magnus cures all of their ills. No charge to the people. If the people of Prali listen and agree with Simon Magnus, they receive free care from their new found leader, their new god.

Hanging upon the local church bell tower, her wrists restrained by rope, her hands tied, hanging in pain. It is the fond friend of Mary. The troops of Magnus patrolled the streets looking for her, going door to door. People witnessed her being with the young man who agreed with Rome. They eventually found her cowering in the home of Mary Archer. Now Simon Magnus questions her in regards to the owner of the home she hid. Magnus can easily get the information from a local. He enjoyed torture. To see a young girl squirm made him joyful. Magnus standing far below the girl while she hangs looks up to her and shouts, "Tell me who lives in that home!" He waits for a response, only to be greeted by spittle falling from the bell tower. "You have till tonight to tell me who lives in that home. If not you will die!" He stands and waits for an answer. Once again spittle hits his left cheek. Magnus walks from under the bell tower and approaches one of his Prali soldiers. "Tell me who lives in the home where this girl hid?" The soldier ready to speak to impress his master says. "That is easy sir. The home belongs to a young girl named Mary Archer." Magnus looks around the room in deep thought. "Why does that name ring a bell with me?" The soldier chuckling towards the comment and says. "No pun intended sir." Magnus finally realizing his mistaken play on words, "Yes I guess you can say that." With a laugh Magnus forgets his thoughts of Mary Archer for now, and returns to focus on the business of Prali.

Bernard and Mary cross the Prali Bridge. They wonder what challenges remain ahead. "Bernie what do you think we will confront in Prali? Look what we have faced so far, a troll from legendary past, something of old fairytales, the loathsome Skulk, who for a second time I killed. What next?" Bernard thought of the questions of the young girl, laughing slightly. "Oh Mary I have no idea, maybe demon fairies." She frowned towards Bernard. "Not funny Bernie, not funny at all." The two friends travelled a short distance, coming towards a small farm. Alone farmer stands on the roadside watching the two young travellers, the two companions approach the farmer who looked pale, and elderly. His hands marred with the look of many years of farming, his clothes tattered and worn. The black boot upon his feet covered in mud. He looks up towards the travellers who ride upon the road, "You one of the agents of Magnus?" Mary stops her steed, along with Bernard and says. "What makes you think we are with Magnus?" The farmer smiles towards the young girl and says. "You don't look like someone who would work for Magnus, and your friend is a monk. Monks or religious are banned from Prali, and soon the entire Turin region." Bernard enters the conversation. "Tell me farmer. Are you an agent of this Magnus?" The farmer smiles and says. "You two get off your horses and water them in my barn. I am no agent of Magnus. My wife has a good supper brewing. Please come and join us. The agents of the night wander the streets patrolling, killing anyone who walks in the dark." The farmer had taken the reins of both horses and guided Mary and Bernard into the barn. Entering the barn the two adventurers dismount their horses and shake the hand of the farmer. "Thank you for your kindness sir." Mary speaking to the farmer in a submissive tone, the farmer blushing, not in the early years of his wife has he seen a girl so innocent and pure of heart.

The farmer escorts the two friends to his humble home, opening his door he shouts. "Anna we have friends for supper!" An elderly female voice shouts in return. "No worries, no worries!" Mary and Bernard are seated in front of a roaring fire, with only candle light upon the table. The three sit and drink. Mary drinking her water, the two men drinking ale. The farmer's wife enters the room placing food upon the table. Roast mutton, cooked potatoes, and carrot stew. The room swept with the smells of a fine meal. The four sit before the fire saying grace. Bernard having the honor of leading the prayer with a simple our father, the four begin to eat. Bernard finally speaks openly and questions. "Tell me farmer. You say agents of Magnus. Please tell us of Prali and the new ruler." The farmer places his hands on the table and speaks of Prali and Simon Magnus. "Prali is now under a dictator. All the beautiful women of Prali are slaves to him. He violates them. Once he tires of them he gives them to his soldiers. He wants to create a world society of his heirs. He wants to be the new Adam. The children are sent to schools of brainwashing. They learn of the greatness of Magnus. The people have no need for shops or goods. He supplies them with all needs. Nobody knows where he gets the food. People say he conjures everything from his hands. People consider him a god. His soldiers are the men of Prali. They serve him well, or die. His soldiers are given a heavens wealth. They have any woman they please, paid in pure gold. Magnus orders them to invade nearby towns and converts the people through conquering them. In the night the roads are patrolled by an unknown evil. People disappear without a trace. The people of Prali are given the Magnus utopia. They have no wants or needs. They live off their lusts and love of Simon Magnus." Mary listens and questions. "Tell me how come you are not affected by Magnus? Everything here seems normal." The farmer looks down to the ground and responds. "Magnus realized I had four young daughters and placed them under arrest. He has done devilish things to them. He considered them payment to continue running my farm. My wife and I are segregated from Prali since we are in the outskirts. Prali pays us no mind." Mary sorrowful to hear the farmer's tale, the monks mind thinking of an approach to this Magnus. Bernard knew who Magnus is and where he originated. Magnus is no dragon, though he isn't one hundred feet tall either. Still Bernard must remind himself how powerful the wizard is, and not to take the wizard for granted.

The four continued with supper and light conversation. After supper the farmer showed Bernard to his room for the night, Mary to hers. That night Mary laid in a bed that once belonged to one of the farmer's daughters. She looked around the room while the candlelight flickered, she was anxious to get to Prali. The next morning the farmer's wife packed the mounts of the priest and the archer with many baked goods for the short ride into Prali. Bernard and Mary thanked the kind farmers and began to ride to face Simon Magnus. Mary looked towards Bernard, asking. "Will you save Prali?" The priest thinking of the question and not sure of himself smiles lightly and says. "We will save Prali."

CHAPTER 7

The Three Avenging Spirits

The snow falling profusely over the Turin province and the little town of Prali, the roads silent, only the light breeze through the streets can be heard. Like a slight murmur of a child's slumber. In the once peaceful church of Prali, Simon Magnus plots his next course of action. Standing by his side is a general from the Persian army. His name is ArAm Raad. Purchased by Magnus and sent to Prali to conduct dominating invasions of local towns near Prali. ArAm trained in the finest arts of Middle Eastern warfare. Fought against many crusader forces in Jerusalem and into the north near the black sea, his muscular build, making up for his short stature, his beard long, and rough like the desert he resides, his armor gold with etchings of crescent moons, his helmet gold with rubies along the top. The invitation from Magnus was unimaginable. How could any man say no to fine jewels, and to fight the Christians. It was the perfect contract for the Persian warrior, and to him and his fellow warriors it seemed a miracle that a white dove would come to him and speak into his ear proclaiming the coming of the wizard. The wizard and the Persian stand over a large map of Italy. ArAm with his arms folded over his gleaming armor of gold, and the wizard with his purple and black cloak, his hand upon his chin looks down towards the map with great interest.

Deep in thought he finally speaks to ArAm. "I have taken Prali and Briancon. We have not heard word from Decorus. We need to send our fighters into Turin and capture the city. There are rumors that Nun's hide the shroud of Jesus, the burial cloth of the son of God. This interests me a great deal. The sword of Peter and the cloth together in my possession, think of it, the world would be mine." ArAm looking intently down towards the map along with Magnus speaks in response. "Yes my lord but there is something else you forget. If you capture the sword, and the cloth, together with the spear that penetrated Christ during the crucifixion, you would control not only the world, but the entire universe. Those three objects have never been combined. The reason for this is because the one who combines them would be all powerful. You could kill or create on a simple thought. The Popes are not even allowed to place all three. The church is aware that even a Pope can be tempted by too much power. This is why they are separated by purpose." Simon Magnus moves his left hand to rest on his servants shoulder. "Yes ArAm you are so correct. This may be possible. The shroud is in Turin. The sword is somewhere in Rome. The spear on the other hand, I have no knowledge." The Persian fighter speaks once more to his master. "I have heard the spear is hiding in the church of the holy sepulcher in Jerusalem. The Catholics and Greek Orthodox keep it safe there. It is protected with armed crusaders and locks. Once we combine the shroud and the sword, the spear will come easy to us." Magnus slowly removes his arm from ArAm's shoulder. "Yes in due time, but first let's focus on taking the lands. We have Prali, and Rome has sent no army. We hear rumors of the French protecting their borders. This is trouble for us since Briancon is actually in French territory. It will be a couple of days before they reach the town of Briancon. ArAm I want you to take your best fighters and find Decorus. Once you find him I want you and he to ride to Briancon and set up defenses against the French. Angrogna should be under the control of Decorus. Take the men of Prali and combine them with the Angrogna men. This should allow you to defeat the French. My magical weapons of power should be enough. My Furiosi protect the roads during the evening. Nothing can challenge my goddesses from hell." Magnus laughing in a sinister tone knowing he now controls parts of northern Italy.

Down in the vastness of the Prali River lays two bodies, Skulk and the troll. A figure of evil hovers over their dead bodies, another figure stands over the body of Skulk. The figure standing over takes its hand and lifts the head of Skulk and says. "This is the servant of Magnus." The dark imagine overhead, with its red eyes and golden hair, her black wings spreading wide, flapping backwards and forwards, speaks in response. "You vampires take the servant and do with him as you wish; he is no good to Magnus. I will inform Magnus of the demise of this thing. He is not what he appears. The wizard ordered us furia to protect this poor excuse for a creature, but we found it in our best interest to stay away from such gutter trash as this. This is his original form before Magnus transformed him into Decorus. Still he may have some use. Not for Magnus, but for your vampire empire." The vampire releases the head of Skulk and says. "I can sense much experience with the darkness in the body of this Decorus, also known as Skulk. I will take him to the underworld and do what must to help in our future war with the world. Let's hope your Simon Magnus can defeat this world before we gain power in our armies. Once he has control of the surface, we will sign our pact with him. He will control the surface and we the underworld. If he fails, we will come and take both surface and the underworld will remain ours." The red eyed golden haired furia nodded her head and responded. "I will inform Magnus. No worries the wizard is taking control more and more every day. Soon this world will pass and the old realm will be renewed." The Furia dressed in black and the pale faced vampire nodded in farewell. The furia racing towards the sky like a shooting star in reverse, the vampire dragging the body of Skulk to the underworld to prepare for the future of the vampire race, with the body of Skulk to be used for their victory, slowly the dark images disappear as swiftly as they appeared. The lone furia is one of three. They are known as the avenging spirits. The first is Alecto the relentless. Eyes red, golden hair, dressed in black. The second furia is Tisiphone the avenger. The third named Megaera the grudge bearer. These three sisters created after the revolt of Satan in heaven. The day Satan fell in battle to Saint Michael is the day the three furia were created. From the underworld they came, now under the control of Simon Magnus and his plans for world domination.

Mary and her companion father Bernard continued forward. Both thinking of the encounter with Skulk and the troll, it pleased Mary; the trickster Skulk was finally deceased. She wanted not a word get out of her romance with such an evil doer. Still it may be an advantage point for her. If Magus knew Mary was involved with Skulk, it may allow her entry to his headquarters, and get close to the wizard. What Mary didn't know is that Magnus was aware of the plan to kill Mary. The two riders only a short distance to the Prali town center, their wariness seen upon their faces. "I forgot how far the Prali Bridge was to the town center." Bernard speaking to Mary, riding together whiles the sun shines upon their faces. The snow hardening into ice, the harshness of an Italian winter on the northern borders thriving and taking over the mountain range, in the distance Mary notices something in the sky. The object some distance away, did not catch the attention of the young girl directly, a passing thought. Until she realized the flying creature was following them. Mary stopped her horse with a light tug of the reins, gazing up towards the sky, her hand slightly over her eyes, blocking the winter sun. Bernard noticing his friend focusing upon the sky, "Is there a problem Mary? Is there something out there?" Mary still looking out and noticing the object becoming closer and closer, the sun making a visual identification almost impossible "Yes father, there is something flying against the wind but I cannot make out what it can be, it is too large to be a bird." Bernard looks towards the direction of Mary's gaze. He sees what has brought her to a standstill. "What do you make of it Mary? It can be anything." The young girl with the trained eyes of her profession continues to watch the object as a cloud slightly blocking the sun, allowing her to get a visual. "Bernard, it is no bird. Besides a bird what else can be flying in the sky? We knew of a dragon, but he is gone from our world. The flying creature is the size of a human. I figure five-four in height." Mary paused, licked her upper lip and continued." It is coming this way." Mary taking her bow in hand prepares for the worst. Bernard realizing his friend is right, loosening his sheath, holding the hilt of his sword. Mary's eyes widen, her jaw drops. "It is a woman, and she has wings." The priest looking closer bringing both his hands to his eyes to block the sun with the passing of the minimal cloud cover, he sees the Furia named Alecto flying towards him, and Mary.

Alecto noticed the two strangers, and followed them a distance. She was on her way to report to Magnus of the news of Skulk. Instead the strangers caught her eye. Approaching the two riders, she noticed the girl on the horse fit a description of a girl Magnus was curious on finding. Alecto knew Magnus was having fun preparing for war and takeovers. She knew his mind was clouded with conquest. Finding the girl was more of a sick game for him, a bit of a hobby. It was an excuse for him to hang Annabella to the church tower, the young Italian girl being captured on the grounds of Mary Archer. Finding the girl made Mary an accomplice to the heresy of Annabella and her dead Fidere. The lone Furia approaches the wide eyed travelers, and hovers before them. Her dark smile gave her intentions away. Alecto did not approach the travelers for conversation, but for confrontation. In her demonic tone she questions the two riders. "I see my nemesis is approaching Prali. Why do you come to this domain of the new god?" Bernard realizing his priestly garments gives him away to the allies of darkness. He never thought of hiding his identity. "Fowl demon we know of no new god. We just know of the one true God." Alecto flapping her wings, the sound echoing, surrounding Bernard and Mary, her power visible to the heroes, her image of fierce evil dominance with fire in her eyes and rage in her heart. "Priest I am not here to converse. I am here to destroy you and your friend. I shall take her for torture and make her a slave to the new world order." Alecto places her hand behind her back, slowly pulling a sword of fire, revealed to all. Flames of gold and red surrounded the long sword. Only an agent of hell can wield such a weapon. The sound of the flickering flame surrounds the area, with the continuous flapping of the wings of the furia. "Now priest I seek vengeance for Skulk, and your head will be my prize."

"Over my dead body you hellish fiend!" The voice of Mary heard loud and clear. Two volleys of Mary's arrows fly towards Alecto. The furia moves slightly to the left realizing the attack, the arrow grazing the golden haired furies' cheek. The second arrow approaches. Alecto swings her sword of fire, incinerating the arrow with the intense heat of her sword. "You have to do better than that little girl!" The furia speaking in a furious tone towards Mary, while the priest watches his friend make the first attack, he pulls his sword from its sheath and jumps from his horse, both hands grasping the hilt. Alecto turns towards Bernard and give an evil chuckle. "You think that little sword can defeat me? Wrong priest, you will die a harsh death and your soul shall be mine for the taking." Alecto diving from her position in the air towards Bernard, her sword held with both hands and in front of her face, the young archer firing more arrows, her second attack incinerating upon impact. The sword of Alecto behind a shield of fire and darkness while she rushes towards Bernard, her eyes becoming angrier with every heartbeat of her dark existence, the force of her flight powerful and unrelenting. The priest never knew of such a creature that approached him for battle. His sword looked weak, tainted with age. The furia had no idea the sword is the weapon of the first Pope Saint Peter, the strongest sword in the history of the world. Bernard rushes towards his enemy, his heart pounds with excitement. Suddenly the sword of Peter and the sword of fire clash. The impact echoing, the fire surrounding Bernard's weapon, the young priest using all his strength, pressing against his sword with all his might, the furies' wings flapping with extreme power. "You shall die Priest." Alecto mocking Bernard as they clash with her evil rage glaring towards the enemy and the priest with his powerful truth and heavenly power from on high. Mary stands and watches the clash, realizing Alecto's back now face her, the furia exposed. Mary launches another round of attacks. Two arrows penetrate the left wing of Alecto, shooting through almost hitting Bernard. The furia realizing the attack from behind slightly turns to face the girl. Bernard noticing the distraction swings his sword against the sword of fire. His sword hitting the top of the furies' weapon and swiftly moving down his opponent's sword, the heavenly weapons sharp point bouncing off the hilt of the furies' sword and severing the hand of Alecto, the severity of the attack, a possible death blow to the evil rogue who was so confident in her victory over the human mortals of this land she hated so much within her heart.

The red eyed furia screams with pain, turning once again to face Bernard. Two more arrows hit Alecto. One in the shoulder blade, blood rushing from her arm and back, the arrow piercing through her neck and protruding from the other end. Severing her vocal cords, the scream less agent of Magnus falls to the ground, her lifeless body slumping over a large stone, the wings lightly fluttering, while the nerves within her body slowly die. Her legs' twitching momentarily, until stillness takes over, and movement ceases, the evil defeated and the creature is sent back to the lower depths of the hellish underworld of Satan and his minions. The priest standing before the dead creature from the underworld, placing his sword back in his sheath, Mary walking over to be by his side while they both look down towards Alecto, she says. "Bernie I don't think this is the usual mission. There is something more evil here than just a dragon. I admit I thought this would be easy compared to the dragon we faced two years ago. This is a whole nothing story. This is something beyond evil." The young priest faces Mary and says. 'You may be right. This Simon Magnus is more experienced than either of us. He has been here since the time of the apostles. We should not underestimate this man, or his minions." Bernard walks over to the furia, taking her hands into his. Looking up to Mary he says. "Come and help me hide the body of this flying demon." Walking over to the furia, Mary grabs the creature's ankles. The two friends carry the demon into the woods and throw her into a river bed, the priest wiping his hands of the furies' blood upon his tunic, the blood of evil staining his holy clothes like the stain upon the soul of humanity and the evil sins of this world.

The border town of Briancon now under the control of Magnus and his minions, nothing left but smoldering buildings and ash, though some of the town remained. The two furies' Tisiphone and Megaera sitting upon a burned out church, Tisiphone with her dark features and identical to her sisters, she turns to Megaera, her long green hair flowing through the wind while ash whispers through the air. Megaera shorter in stature than her sisters of the furia, dressed identical, except for her purple hair, and blood dripping from her tear duct. "Where is our sister? She should have been here to meet us?" Megaera looking into the distant sky, hoping to see a glimpse of Alecto's return responds. "I feel in my heart that something is amiss. She is never delayed. I fear something, but not sure. Maybe it is my own uncertainty. We must remain here till ArAm comes to Braincon and secures this town for Magnus. The French may arrive soon, and we are the only defense." Tisiphone looks forward and wonders where her sister may be. The furies are fierce and show no mercy, hoping for a fight, and conflict. In the hearts of the sisters, they hope the French will arrive.

ArAm the fierce general rode towards the south of Italy to find Decorus. Seven hundred men followed, equipped with short and long swords. A small army created to chop and hack, and destroy. The army now only a short distance from the location of the priest and the archer, their steeds hooves trudging through the snow of the Turin province. Can a priest and an archer win against seven hundred strong, experienced warriors? In the sky approaching ArAm a black crow originating from the stronghold of Simon Magnus with a message or a possible change of strategy for the army made for destruction. The Persian general noticed the dark bird, raising his hand to the sky to halt his army. The sound of approaching warriors ceased with the silence of the clanging armor. ArAm's hand remained lifted towards the heavens. The crow landing upon his fist, with a small parchment attached to the talons. The general releasing the parchment from the crow drops his arm, while the crow lifts off and fly's back to Magnus. The Persian opens the scroll and reads the careful message from his master. He studies the words and once read, turns to his men throwing the parchment to the soft wet ground beneath his horse's hooves, "Warriors of Magnus!" He shouts. "I have received word that our mission has changed. We will turn away from Angroga, and move our strength towards Briancon!" The warriors lifted their swords and screamed for victory. ArAm moved his horse towards the town of Briancon and headed North West.

Bernard and Mary mounted their steeds and prepared once more towards Prali. In the distance the young archer could see a small army of warriors, only images and shadows, no details to be seen from such a long distance. Bernard noticed the warriors, while the two friends watched the small army move westward. "What do you think of that Bernie, looks like we are in the perimeter of the whore of Babylon?" The Francisca looking forward, his mind set on the mission, his face grim with sorrow. "Mary, we must be cautious. This is worse than any dragon or evil creature. We are going up against the greatest evil, and destructive creatures ever created. We are going against pure evil men corrupt by power." The girl smiles and says. "Finally we agree. Men are the worst creatures ever created." Bernard perked up his head at the girl's confident response to the dangers ahead. The two adventurers kicking the sides of their horses and riding forward into the town of Prali, the priest knowing this would be a daunting task. To unseat a creature like Magnus from the grip he holds on Prali. The victory of Angroga was child's play compared to Prali. Skulk was a push over and just a servant of evil. Bernard still wondered why Mary was so hushed over Skulk. Why did she act secretive? The Monk decided to question Mary. "Can you tell me why you disregarded Skulk and threw him off the bridge?" Mary now realizing Bernard was doing a friendly interrogation responded. "It is obvious why. He was killed before and he lived. He returns to the world in the form of this Decorus. To make sure he was dead was the right course." Bernard thinking of the words of his friend responds. "Yes, but it would have been better to burn his body, and turn him into ash. Ashes to ashes, dust to dust." Mary speaking with a nervous tone replies. "I suppose you're right about it. I was not thinking. My first thought was to destroy. My adrenaline was pumping. You forget I am just seventeen." Bernard thinking of the words of Mary, buying her words, hook, line, and sinker, he knew she had a good heart, just an average teenager.

The two companions riding closer to Prali, until they reach a small sign on the side of the snow burdened dirt road. The sign read, "Welcome To Prali." In the distance the entry into the town could be seen. The roof tops visible, the church cross upon the steeple ever present. No people to be seen, no movement, just silence. Only the sound of the light winter wind being heard, the sun now turning towards the Prali mountain tops, and ceasing to the evening shadows. The moon slowly rising towards the stars, a new night now in command of the western province, the bird slumbers while the snake rattles in the darkness. Where will this mission lead Bernard and Mary? They now ride into the hands of Simon Magnus and his new Prali. ArAm and his warriors of seven hundred race to Briancon to defend against a possible French assault, the last two furies' upon the earth waiting patiently for some sign of their sister, and word from Magnus. Now the wizard sits upon the church altar in Prali, Annalisa still hanging like a church bell within the church of the old magician. Her wrists purple from the rope restraints. Now forces will meet, and only one will be victorious. The evil of heresy and lust, against the ethical moral beliefs of a priest and his innocent young friend, the stars now peering and shining towards the earth below, the moon light now covering the world into shadow, Darkness has arrived, and Magnus is at his peak of power. His one goal is to make himself a god and to eliminate anyone who opposes him. Magnus is the power of evil on earth. Taking the scepter of Satan in his hands, and raising it against God and the people, he is sure of his victory and nobody can stop him from his evil destruction.

CHAPTER 8

The Culture War

Night takes over Italy; the two friends on horseback continue to ride towards the town of Prali. Before entering the town center, Mary knew they would ride past her home. She wanted to check on her friend Annalisa, the girl who lost her Fiancé to the hordes of Magnus followers. Mary also felt saddened and uneasy about her home. She wondered if it still stood. Bernard and Mary riding past the Prali homes, and finally riding directly to the home of the young English girl, the closer they rode into town, the more homes surrounded them. Mary stops in front of her home, turning to face the front door of the Old Italian style home while the priest rode forward towards town center. No candle light in the house. Only the moonlight shined upon her home. Giving the look of ominous despair, Bernard noticed Mary was not following him. He stops and turns, the young girl staring at the door of the Italian abode. "Mary is there a problem with this road?" Bernard realizing she is having a concern for this certain home. He turns his horse and his attentions towards her, riding to her side. In a still voice he speaks. "Mary you ok, you are not looking well? We need to continue and rest before morning. We have Magnus to confront." The girl looking deep within her soul, only the door took her mind away from the world. Then she hears the voice of the Franciscan and responds. "Oh I am sorry my friend. This is my home. I left my friend here to hide from the men of Magnus. Her Fiancé died trying to protect her from the men of Magnus. Noticed no light be flickering, I wondered if she is alive or dead. My home doesn't seem to be out of sorts." Bernard realizing the importance, said to Mary. "We must go inside and find out if your friend is alive or not. It is also a good place to rest before we confront Magnus." Mary nodded in agreement and dismounted her horse, tying the ropes adjacent to the reins to a tree. Bernard followed her lead, and walked behind her while she cautiously approached her own front door.

Mary slightly pushes the door with her left hand, the door creaking while it opens. The peering moonlight shining upon the room within the home, the moonlight revealing what Mary feared. The house had been completely ransacked by intruders. Mary walks over to a candle lying on the floor and places the candle on a holder. Bernard looks over the room while Mary strikes two daggers together, to cause sparks. She kneels before her fireplace, and eventually the sparks created by the friction of the two daggers causes the fireplace to ignite, the archer places wood in the fireplace, walking back towards the candle to light it. The fire light brings out more answers to the destroyed home. Bernard turning to Mary says. "Looks like several marauders have come and gone since you left." The monk continuing to rummage through his friends belongings on the floor, the entire house was overturned. Chairs thrown against the wall, parchments, the bed, tables. Mary looks for Annalisa, but no sign, not even her body. Mary clinches her fists in anger. "This is war Bernard. How dare they come to my home and destroy it." Her anger in her eyes told her thoughts, the priest realizing her tension and her feeling of her privacy being invaded. He responded to her with a calm tone. "Mary since they have come to your home and tossed things about it tells me that they are looking for something, maybe looking for you." Mary walked over to the door leading to her bedroom and said. "They will find me friend. I will make myself known and there is nothing you can do. We will finish this mission with victory." The Priest felt the confidence of the young girl pouring out of her.

The invasion of the girl's home did not depress her like the enemy hoped. It made her stronger. Many memories filled the girls mind. Her mother, and father, the times they shared. The enemy made their mistake, and the girl was ready to win at all costs.

Walking into her bedroom Mary pushed the wooden framed bed to the side. A simple bed made from local carpenters in Prali. The bed moving slowly with the grunts of the young girl as she pushes with all her strength, under the bed a small door revealed. Taking her sword from her sheath, she places it in the small crack between the wooden floor and the wooden door. Lifting the sword slightly under the secret door, and lifts, the door becomes ajar, while the girl pushes the door to the side, behind the small door, a room only big enough for a small child of a skinny Dwarf. Mary jumps in the room feet first. Bernard thinking the girl is a genius having a trap door with a small room. Now he watched the door, while he heard noise from beyond the revealed door. Eventually the young girls hand would pop out from the door, arrows being placed on the floor. Mary had been hiding weapons, her secret stash. More arrows appeared and a crossbow, silver and golden pointed arrows, daggers, mini crossbow. Mary was prepared for the end of the world. To the young girl, now was the end of the world. Now she was preparing to defeat the menace, and restore her life to normal conditions. Lifting herself from her hidden fortress of destruction, she begins to pick up her weapons, and strap them to her body. First the variety of arrows, the mini crossbows on each hip, crossbow strapped to her back along with her bow, daggers placed adjacent to the mini crossbows. The young girl now prepared for war, turning to finally face Bernard. The priest standing in the bedroom doorway with his arms crossed. "You ready Mary?" He questions the young girl with shock and awe. Mary winked innocently and responds by simply saying. "Let's do this."

The snow ceased, the winter clouds begin to part, and the stars slowly begin to peer in the night's sky. Above the French town of Briancon a small army observes the ruined town. The armor of the men shined upon the revealed stars. One man stood before the others, the leader of the troops. His name is Clement Laurent, a French captain, and a mighty warrior. He served France since he was of military age, and served to perfection. The banners of France beside him, glowing the colors of blue and yellow from the starlight, his brown hair slightly blowing in the mild breeze, his unshaven face, and his deep hazel eyes only shadows, while the stars shine above him, his men sit upon their steeds waiting for his orders. The French captain leads a small army of five hundred French soldiers. In Paris, France the government received reports on the attack of Briancon, and the word of a mysterious wizard. Clement was given the duty to search for this wizard, and to secure Briancon for the banner of France. The King of France also received word from the Pope, and both decided to combine forces against the wizard named Simon Magnus. Clement noticed nothing in the town, it was under complete darkness. "Sir shall we enter Briancon?" One of the men holding the French banner questioned. Clement stared forward into the darkness and said. "Briancon was a place of peace. A mountain town filled with love and laughter, now nothing comes from it, just blackness." Clement paused in thought, his mind occupied; he continued to answer his banner man. "Yes my friend we shall go down into Briancon and see what is left. Warn the men to be guarded, something doesn't seem right. We have no idea what lurks in the town below. Is it nothingness, or does the enemy awaits us, and attack." Clement raising his fist towards the stars closes his fist, a signal to his men to move forward into Briancon. The smell of burnt wood and ash made the captain uneasy.

The two furies' resting peacefully upon the burnt out church await word from Magnus, when suddenly Tisiphone notices something moving from atop the mountain side, her keen perfect eyesight looking towards the glare caused by the star light. She turns to her sister Megaera, and announces her find, "Looks like we have some visitors, images of troops of some kind." Megaera stands from her position and steadies her balance against the burnt cross atop the church. "It is an army, and not friendly." The two furia sisters observe the enemy, the still darkness being their camouflage. Tisiphone the avenging furia thinks of a plan of defense, but her sister Megaera the grudge furia thinks of a plan of ambush, Tisiphone, the first to speak. "Allow us to hide in the shadows and observe this threat. If they are passing by we shall ignore them and continue to wait for word of Magnus. Megaera laughs, responding. "Don't be foolish, these are warriors. You know they are here to investigate the destruction of the town. Allow us to wait in hiding, and then attack them by surprise." Tisiphone thought of her sisters words. She knew an ambush would be folly, but she enjoyed the idea, and her evil thoughts got the best of her. "Ok Meg, allow us to ambush these bastards. We will show them what we have in store for them." The sisters give each other a devilish smile, and jump from the ruins of the church. Tisiphone placed herself behind an old well the town folk used to fetch water. Megaera ran to an old abandoned bakery. Both the furies stood in the darkness awaiting the French troops. The French entered Briancon from the west, while something new entered the town.

From the east of Briancon arrived ArAm and his seven hundred soldiers equipped with swords and heavy armor, their horses trudging through the hard ice below them. Nothing survived in Briancon after the arrival of Simon Magnus. Once was a place of great joy, now was a dark dessert of burnt destruction, not even the animals survived, no stone was unturned for Magnus on that fateful day he arrived with Skulk. ArAm and his men knew of the details of the destruction of Magnus, but seeing the destruction first hand amazed them. It was dark for the men, the shadows revealing the destruction with the starlight overhead. The army of Magnus continued through the darkness until they reached the church. The two furia, Tisiphone and Megaera noticed the men, but remained silent. They giggled under their breath, knowing what laid ahead for ArAm and his men. The furia loved to be entertained, especially by mortal humans. ArAm turned to his right hand man and said. "Magnus said the furia would be here waiting for us. It seems these hell demons decided to leave for something more interesting. It was their job to secure these lowly remains of a town." The soldier responded to his leader. "Sir, I know not of the habits of these beasts. I just know what is before my eyes, and I see nothing but burnt ruins." ArAm confused about the situation, sitting upon his horse.

Clement Laurent riding into town noticed the cross above the church and said. "Men we shall ride to the cross!" For the French the cross was a sign of safety, and faith. The French riding ever closer to the church and towards the seven hundred warriors who followed ArAm and who worked for the wizard, the warriors in their minds knew wizards are created by evil, but the money offered was too good to pass up. The armor of the Magnus force was grey and dark, perfect for nightfall. The French always found pride in clean armor shining bright. Unfortunately the French respected their armor more than their own bodies. Armor was cleaned nightly, their bodies monthly. The echoes of the French armor being heard through the town. ArAm knowing the sound all too well announced to his men. "Prepare for battle!" The men of Magnus formed two groups in front of the church, only two hundred able to fit in the church square. The other men sat upon their horses on an adjacent street, the French riding into town towards the church in rows of ten. Clement noticed the sound of soldiers ahead, and eventually he spotted an outline of men on horseback in the church square. He lifted his hand, raising one finger in the air, the signal to equip weapons and prepare for battle. The French prepared by taking their swords from their sheaths, and placing them in hand. The French troops halting adjacent to the church and on the other side of the square, the men of Magnus. The two leaders of soldiers noticed each other. Clement Laurent looking into the eyes of ArAm Raad, the Saracen fiend the first to speak, "What brings the French to the once was Briancon?" The words simple and straight to the point, Clement answered the question with a forceful tone. "Briancon is in French territory, and under French control." ArAm spoke defiant. "Sorry to inform you that Briancon now belongs to lord Simon Magnus, god on earth. I suggest you inform your king of this change in leadership." Clement tightened his grip upon his sword and said.

"Sorry to inform you, but this is still French control, and your master is no god but a fraud." ArAm feeling his heart pound faster responded. "Well sir it seems we have a disagreement, and must decide this by battle." ArAm lifted his sword up to the night sky and yelled "Attack!" ArAm and his two hundred rushed on horseback towards Clement and the French troops. The French did their best to fit every man into the square to face the men of Magnus, the captain riding towards the enemy with his men.

The men of Magnus and the French now in conflict, the furies salivated towards the excitement and entertainment or mortals from the surface world fighting for their lives. Clement ordered his men to advance, ArAm and his men continued to charge, both armies charging towards one another, silence falling upon the land and the ruins of Briancon, only the sound of men and horse hooves. Suddenly a deafening sound of sword and armor clashing between one another, the pain of horses slamming into each other, while their masters battle before the ruined church. Clement Laurent surrounded by a blur of armor, and swords, not realizing his sword had entered into the enemy during impact. Two opponents remained to his left and right. Both taking their swords and attacking Clement. The French leader ducks his head avoiding one of the attackers, his sword blocking the attack of the other. His ears ringing with the sound of battle, his horse turning towards the attacker who missed his target, the head of the horse bashing into the horse of the enemy, the evil warrior caught off his guard, while his horse jumped on his hind legs. The warrior falling to the muddy ground, being stomped by the other surrounding horses involved in the conflict, the other warrior raising his sword towards Clement, only to be blocked once more by the French leader. Clement swinging his sword after the block, the attack hitting the mark, the evil villain falling to the ground, his head separating from the body, landing on the ground while two more attackers came towards Clement, his sword swinging with no control blocking his attackers, The captains horse slamming its body into the other steeds, the sound of clashing metal, the fall of the men surrounding Clement. His troops were gaining the upper hand while more of the men of Magnus filled the void of the fallen. The dead being crushing into the soaked winter ground of Briancon.

ArAm leading the charge feeling a rip of armor flying from his shoulder, a French soldier penetrating his armor with a lance, ArAm raising his sword in the air, striking the mighty French jouster as the body limps and falls to the ground, a small victory for the evil leader. This warrior from the Middle East has never been so overwhelmed in battle, his first experience against the French soldiers. ArAm defeating every Frenchmen who attacks him, they fall to his sword, lambs to the slaughter. One man caught the eye of ArAm while the battle raged around him. The smell of fresh blood began to take over the scent of the sundered town. ArAm raced towards this man who slain every man that approached him. He fought his way through the clashing of swords to reach the French leader, who found himself on the steps of the church overlooking the remaining battle. The darkness of the evil ones begins to fall to the banner of the French colors. ArAm needed no words to show Clement his challenge; words were already spoken before battle. Now it is time for the two leaders to clash, and mingle their swords, and possibly their blood. Clement turns to face a racing ArAm. Their swords clashing, the sweat on their brows showed the struggle between the two men, both with a purpose and a reason for victory. The furies witnessing the men of Magnus fall to the French. The narrow road working in the favor of the well-equipped men of the west, and experts at their craft of war, the grunts and the sound of struggle are heard from the cold breath of Clement and ArAm. The leader of evil being pushed back by Clement, the French being too much for the ill equipped evil, ArAm knowing this battle is now over, and in need of retreat. His voice rang out, words he thought he would never leave his lips, "RETREAT!!!!" ArAm turning from Clement while he rode away from the battle, the road not so filled with warriors, just dead men in armor, and bleeding horses.

The remaining men of Magnus scatter through the town, the French troops willing to pursue, only to be called off by Clement; other troops take their colors and raising their banners in victory yelling. "Victory is ours!" The furies watch in horror, seeing the allies of ArAm and the Perisans defeated. Both Tisiphone and Megaera streaking towards the sky, Clement witnessing their hasty departure with a shocking grimace upon his face. "What was that my lord?" One of the French soldiers questioning his leader, Clement responding with hesitation and heavy breathing, his mind swirling in disbelief of what he had just seen take flight. "I have no idea my friend. I have a bad feeling we will find out sooner or later." The French now began the long task of burying the dead of both armies. ArAm and his men rode in the darkness back to the town of Prali fearing the French would be in pursuit close behind. What ArAm Raad didn't understand is that the French always bury their dead. He knew Magnus would not be please, and he feared for his own life. His mind confused from the battle, not understanding the defeat. He thought of the furia, and wondered what may have happened to them. Did the enemy defeat them? Did they make it to Briancon? He knew not of their whereabouts. He would be on a rampage if he knew they were watching the battle with eyes of pleasure. To see men in battle excited the evil furia, they could not help but to reach ecstasy of the battle. The French raised their flag in the town center of Briancon, Clement shouting. "Briancon belongs to France!" His men cheering, the sound of victory comes to Briancon, and is now free once more, the settlement will be rebuilt and freedom once more will return.

Bernard and Mary retrieve what is left of the weapons from the home of Mary. The two friends placing their boots upon the stirrups and tightening their grip upon their horses reins. The Priest glances towards his young friend, and says. "You ready to ride into Prali?" He thought he was only a right hand man to the young girl. She now seems to be in control of this mission, the girl now lives with a personal purpose to see the death of Magnus and his men. Mary kicked her horse without a word and continued towards the main street of Prali. The town was dark with only a few candles in the window. In times of war candles in a window was a message for soldiers, meaning safe haven. The two adventurers traveled slowly through town. Nothing to be seen, the chimney smoke covered the sky, coming closer to the town center, and the location of the church controlled by Magnus. Suddenly Mary, with her keen eye sight noticed two men standing on the main road. Both dark figures with double sided axes, wearing black hoods, the archer and the monk stopped before approaching the two figures. While one of the men asked a question towards the two friends. "What brings you to Prali?" The sinister tone of the man's voice brought chill upon the skin of the young girl, she rode closer to the figures who interrogated. "I am a citizen of Prali, and this is a priest from Rome." Mary's answer to the men made Bernard uneasy. He thought it a mistake to give the men so much information.

The two guards of Prali looked upon the girl and the priest. Their response was not one of friendship. "My dear girl, priests are forbidden in this region. Only the rule of Magnus applies. Now come down from your horses before we decide to throw you down." The two guards lifting their swords from their hilts and aiming them towards the two heroes. Bernard turned his head slightly to Mary and said. "What do you propose we do, seems like another fight is in order?" Mary with fire in her eyes, her mind still focused on her home. "Sorry Bernard, there is no quarter for these lads. If they won't move I shall run them down." Bernard shocked by the words of his companion. The archer turns towards the guards and supplies them with the stern warning to move or be trampled. The guards laughing at the young girls jest. "My dear you are too innocent to do such things. Now come let us take care of your needs personally, since you seem to be need of a man." Mary angry towards the arrogance of the guard who spoke in haste, kicking the side of her horse, while her horse bucked forward in a rush the Franciscan follows the lead of his revengeful friend. The eyes of the guards opened wide while they turned to flee. Within second the crushing of their bones being heard under the heels of Mary and Bernard.

The trampled bodies of the guards lay cold in the snow and mud of the Prali streets. Mary looking back, her heart feeling no remorse for the two men she killed, her heart has grown cold. With the death of her mother, her home, the sight of Prali being controlled by a mad man, all these things brought her to the harsh reality of a woman. No longer a child she is growing into a warrior of no mercy.

Bernard noticed in the distance the cross atop the steeple. The two friends rode towards the church while the moonlight gleamed upon their faces, making way for shadows, and images of the night that only the moonlight can conjure. The priest and the archer sitting upon their steeds look up towards the large church doors, the chill of the north Italian wind growing slightly stronger as it brushes across the young girls face, her focus on the task at hand. The church steps seemed to go on forever up towards heaven, in the distance the doors of the church. Only the moonlight aided them in their visual. Slightly the door opens; a hand slightly creeps from between the two doors from the inside. The door opens fully to expose the one behind the massive wooden doors. Standing before Mary and Bernard, the one called Simon Magnus. In his hands a wooden staffs with a purple crystal orb resting atop of the magical weapon. Magnus peered towards Mary and said. "You must be the girl who slayed the dragon. I remember you only as a vision within my head. I can hear the battle in my mind. I was the one encased in ice where your battle had taken place. I know you observed me, how can you not notice me? You killed the dragon and his servant. Though you ignored the old man dressed in purple. How Christian is it to not help your fellow man? You are a hypocrite, along with your monk friend, or shall I call him priest?"

The two companions look up towards the wizard, the wizard of Prali. Bernard taking the lead, takes one step closer to Magnus, and says. "Magnus we are here to set order to the region. We are here on orders of the Pope, come with us and avoid conflict." The priests voice calm and relaxed while anger spreads through the veins of the wizard while he replies. "You two fools found luck against the dragon, but now you will fall against god on earth." His words spoke with anger, his eyes glowing red. Magnus remembered the last priest who brought him down and he made a pact within himself that it will never happen again. "Die you heathens!" Magnus shouting his words while his hands begin to glow. A light purple color surrounding his hands, matching his purple robe, and black trim, his white beard seemed to glow with power in the light forming around his hands. The purple glow forming a ball around his hands, with one whispering word from the lips of Magnus, the balls launch towards Mary and Bernard.

The ball of purple racing towards targeted heroes, racing towards them, the girl having no time to take her bow and arrow in hand, leaps to the side, avoiding the attack. The Franciscan taking his sword, swinging it towards the purple attack, striking the magical glow, the attack of Magnus surrounds the sword, and swirls lightly, until it dissipates into nothingness. Bernard pointing the sword towards Magnus, while Mary jumps up from her crouched position, dusting herself off with her delicate hands. Simon Magnus looks at the sword, while his jaw drops to the ground. He recognizes this sword held by the priest, the sword of the first Pope, Saint Peter. The same sword that Saint Bernard used to defeat him so long ago, the same sword used by Peter to strike down the enemies of the lord in the garden. This time Simon Magnus will not fail, and he will defeat the weapon that imprisoned him so many years ago.

Bernard realizes his chance to strike Magnus while the wizard is stunned over the failed attack. He begins to charge towards the enemy, while archer pulls her bow from her back, and places an arrow in position. Mary's first arrow whizzes past the ear of Bernard, while the young priest continues his charge. The wizard seeing the two friends make their move slightly leaps left to avoid the arrow screaming towards him. With a snap of his fingers a purple dome surrounds Magnus, along with Bernard. Magnus smiles and yells towards the young English girl. "Lass I have created a force field that no arrow can penetrate!" Now only Bernard has the opportunity to attack. The wizard now twirling his hands and creating a glowing green whip conjuring it from thin air, moving his hands in a pushing motion the green glowing whip swirls towards the charging Bernard. The whip hitting the Franciscans ankles, and wrapping around his feet causing him to fall at the feet of Magnus with a thump, his head hits the edge of the church steps making a bloody gash upon his temple knocking him out instantly. Simon Magnus taking the sword from the hands of the fallen Bernard while his laughter fills the night sky, the young girl stunned while her mind races to find answers to defeat the wizard. "I have the sword of Peter! I shall rule the world, and make it my footstool." The young archer witnessing her friend fall to his knees while the wizard takes the sword into his hands gloating with great passion of his easy victory, his arrogance ever present with a boosted ego.

Suddenly the force field lowers and Magnus moves towards Mary Archer. Before the girl can continue another attack two warriors under the control of Magnus takes her arms and twists them into her back, her bow falling to the ground, her lips giving way to a painful groan. Simon Magnus tapping his middle finger to his chin smiles and says to Mary. "Your friend is no use to us. He has no power to defeat me, or a baby lamb for that matter. You will come with us to Saint Bernard's pass. The same location you defeated the dragon. I will place you on the altar with nothing to bear upon your body. I will make you a sacrifice, the first of my new empire. Once my magic is performed upon you, you will be killed and sent to your maker. You and your friend had no chance, why bother with your mission of folly?" Before Mary could speak a response one of the warriors hits her on the back of the head knocking her out cold. Magnus looks at both his prisoners and gives his orders to his men. "Leave the priest here to rot and allow the people to take him and string him up upon a tree. Come with me and take the girl with us. You are not allowed to touch her in anyway. I must have her pure and innocent to complete the summoning of the reign of terror upon earth." The two men strapped Mary upon a horse while Magnus walked along the road out of Prali, and towards the pass of Saint Bernard.

CHAPTER 9

Repentance of Prali

The cool misty air of a winter's night in Prali, the priest lying face down upon the ground of the Italian village, his body feeling the sting of defeat, and despair. Slightly shadows move around him while the dark clouds move and separate before the moon. The beaten hero regains his thoughts and is thinking of his errors wondering how he could have lost his battle with Magnus and where would he have gone. Mary was nowhere to be seen. It was obvious Magnus had taken her for prisoner and looking at the direction of the horse hooves indented into the moist ground it was not difficult to know exactly how to track the wizard. The young priest realized at this moment the weakness of Magnus, it was his arrogance. The wizard had no thought of disguising or hiding the tracks of his horse or to eliminate his enemy at once. Lifting his body from the cold ground he stands resolute, prepared for the quest to track his enemy and to rescue his dear friend Mary Archer. The people of Prali looked at Bernard through their windows and creaking doors. Some of the guards of Prali even noticed the monk. They all began to walk towards him. The Franciscan priest stood his ground expecting a fight for survival against the people. Instead the people walked towards him with open arms, even the guards did the same. One of the older women of Prali approached Bernard and fell to the ground asking for forgiveness. All of Prali began to come to Bernard requesting the same as the old woman. One of the guards stood next to the priest and said. "Forgive Prali father, we were forced to follow the wizard. We had two choices, to follow the wizard of die from his tormented evil magic." The Franciscan glared and responded. "You people took the wizard into your arms, you did nothing." The guard defended his words by saying. "Father his magic controls the mind, he can control an entire village. What looked like acceptance was actually mind control." Bernard looked into the eyes of each and every individual who surrounded him. Looking into their souls, their eyes windows, he looked inward into them. The people kneeled and asked the priest for repentance. The priest lifted his right hand, and prayed for the souls surrounding him. The act of contrition spoken from the lips of the people while they hang their heads in humility and their heads bowed to the ground. Prali has returned to innocence.

ArAm rode swiftly with his fighters back to Prali, their armor stained with the blood of defeat. In the distance ArAm could see the town of Prali. He heard shouts of joy, shouts of freedom. ArAm raised his fist to order a halt of his men. The fighters of Magnus listened while Prali rejoiced in their new found freedom. The power of wizardry was dissipating, the farther he removed himself from Prali, the weaker his influence was in the region. Briancon was won by the French, but if Magnus would have remained in the town, the French would have lost, and their bodies crushed by the power of the evil one. Not only was arrogance a weakness of the wizard, but also the power to maintain control was just as weak. Magnus never realized that once he left a region his power left with him. How could he ever know such things. Surrounding him was power, how could he not know, he had never left himself. All these years the power consumed him and he never understood the fullness of the power. In his visionary mind he was powerful, but beyond himself laid little power. He never thought outside himself. Magnus was not the only one to be blinded by power. Anyone with any type of power can fall into folly. From the smallest baker who owns his business from the Pope who is the most influential person on earth. Anyone who controls the lives or finances of people can lose control, and consume themselves with power. It is sad but the majority of people become consumed.

ArAm looked at his men and said. "We will ride into Prali and retake her for Magnus." Second in command turned to ArAm and responded. "Sir this is not our faith, not our lands. We need to return to the mid-east, return to Allah." ArAm smiled and said. "Yes you are right my brother, but first lets dip our swords in Christian blood. The only good Christian is a dead one, and once we send the Christians to their maker we will kill every infidel who crosses our path." The second in command looks upon ArAm with disappointment and responds. "Sir we have few men now. The French has decimated our numbers. You are talking suicide." ArAm with a grim look of determination says, "No my brother we will be rewarded in heaven." ArAm raising his sword to the heavens and orders his men in a thunderous voice. "Onward to victory my Saracen brothers!" ArAm and his band of fighters rush onward towards the town of Prali, in search of victory, in search of honor.

Some of the people in the outskirts of Prali noticed the riders of Magnus, with ArAm in the lead. The people organized as best as they could. Swords, whips, and pitchforks, even Bernard noticed the rushing enemies of Prali. The invaders entered the town heading towards the town center; the people charged the men of Magnus. ArAm arrived in the town center with Bernard standing before them. ArAm sitting upon his horse raising his sword and pointing it towards the priest, "You are the one who converts the town belonging to Magnus?" The priest laughed at the words of ArAm, and responded. "No my friend, it was the people who converted themselves back to the proper calling." The monk looked around him noticing the entire town surrounding the small band of fighters lead by ArAm. Suddenly without hesitation the town engulfed the eastern warriors like a hurricane. The fighters being thrown from their steeds, ArAm hitting the ground, his armor making his reaction slow and limited. The people strike ArAm and his men without mercy, the priest walking away from the fight and turning his back from the chaos. Two men held down the hands of ArAm, his feet also held, while ArAm lay upon the ground forced to endure the stripping of his armor. He yelled in anger while he lay without protection or his dark armor, all his weapons in the hands of his villager assassins. Suddenly ArAm feels a sword penetrate is abdomen, and then another, Blood gushing and flowing like a red river. A dagger shoved through his neck, axes cutting off his legs. The people tearing ArAm into several pieces. Blood covered the town center with only the sounds of dying screaming men and flowing blood of the eastern warriors. ArAm and his men ripped into several bits and eventually thrown into a large bonfire, the smell of burnt flesh consuming the town center while piles of human remains are piled for incineration, the people looking towards the future with new hope. What ArAm planned against the people of Prali had been done to him in the end and his life forfeited. He was the one who was killed without mercy. The killing of ArAm and his men became so legendary in the area that no human army ever invaded after the day of the killing of ArAm and his men.

Bernard continued to walk away from the carnage of human debris. He looked onward towards the road ahead, his mission now set upon the rescue of his friend. Bernard looks at the tracks of the horses and ponders if he is ready for the task of confronting Simon Magnus. It was him and wizard nobody else stood in the way. The power of Magnus lifted from Prali like a morning fog. It was time for Bernard to set out and rescue Mary from the clutches of evil. The young priest located his horse and rode back to the home of Mary where he would set his plan into motion. Upon entering the home of his English friend, it felt dark and filled with the shadow of evil. Bernard remembered where Mary kept her war chest and rummaged through her weapons. His eyes observing every detail of each weapon, he wanted to be prepared and his mind was filled with a solution of rescue and not of vengeance. He knew he had to be pure of heart to win against evil. One will never be victorious if victory is won by doing deeds of evil. He places a sword in his sheath, daggers in both boots, and holy water secured in his pouch. Bernard lifted himself from war chest, and walked towards the front door of the home. He turns and says, "You shall return to your home Mary, I promise thee." With those words he mounts his horse and rides through the darkness uttering a simple prayer. "Although I walk in a darksome valley, I shall fear no evil, for thou art with me. Thy crook and thy staff, these comfort me."

Tisiphone and Megaera sat in a meadow; their bodies covered in snow, their evil eyes peer from the darkness. The two furia are in conference over the situation at hand. Tisiphone moves her hands to the ground, her palms pressing on the wet muddy ground. Her hands reaching beneath the snow, her eyes begin to roll behind her head while she searches for her sister Alecto. The body of Tisiphone shakes in anger while she receives word from hell and the lands beyond the universe. "My word sister Megaera, I have words of distress. I should return to Tartarus and guard the realms of evil. We have lost in this world my sister. Alecto has been defeated, and has been sent back home to our maker." Megaera turns her evil eye towards her sister and says. "I knew this my sister I can feel it. Alecto surrounds me as we speak of her. She tells me to find revenge for her." Tisiphone digs her hands deeper into the earth, her wings tucked tight behind her back. Moments of silence, then Tisiphone speaks to her sister with the answers they searched for. "My sister it seems that Alecto was sent back by a priest and a young English girl. In my mind I felt the sting of battle. Our sister was cheated, her enemies nothing more than backstabbers. I suggest we hunt down these two heathens and bring them to hell with us. Once we destroy them on earth we can lay claim to their souls. Once in our grasp in hell we can torture them as we wish for all eternity." With the words of Tisiphone the two furies grin and laugh at the thought of victory.

Bernard rode slowly making sure not to miss the tracks upon the rocks that hide the evidence of a scoundrel and his escape. He notices the tracks leading in the direction of Saint Bernard Pass. There was so much land to cover and so little time. The priest thought to himself and wondered if the wizard was heading to the location of the defeated dragon and past imprisonment. Bernard wasn't sure if he should lay all his eggs in one basket and rush to the pass. The town of Prali was now in the distance behind him and only the dark forests and mountain passes before him. The snow began to drift downwards resting lightly on his shoulders. The priest took comfort within his heart that Prali was now free from Magnus and he knew to keep it free he must defeat the ancient foe. He also thought of his innocent friend Mary and her dilemma. He felt that he was riding to face the wizard for the rescue of his friend more than the freedom of Prali and the world. The moonlight begins to fade while the thick winter clouds begin to blur out the moon. Snow slightly increasing while the monk moves forward into the darkness. He follows the tracks to a frozen pond noticing that his foe had rested near the water's edge. The Franciscan dismounts his steed and looks towards the ground, no signs of struggle. He wondered if his friend was still alive. He lowers himself on bended knee and begins to pray for knowing the location of Simon Magnus. His praying became so intense he felt not the cold air upon his face or the snowfall upon his shoulders. In the back of his conscience three words came to him, "Saint Bernard Pass." Opening his eyes he now felt confident to follow the sign within his mind. The pass would be his destination.

Not far from where the lone priest investigated the whereabouts of his friend the wizard and his guards stop to rest their horses. The young girl strapped to a horse, her feet and hands bound, her mouth gagged. Simon Magnus investigated the area along with his two guards. "Place the girl on the ground against the tree." The wizard orders his men. The two guards take Mary from her unpleasant position on the horse and place her on the ground. Mary kicks and screams but all in vein. One of the guards walks over to the wizard and asks. "My lord what shall we do for you?" Magnus turns slightly towards the guard and responds with his index finger running across his chin. The wizard was in deep though. "My friend you serve me and I give you pleasures beyond your comprehension. You enjoy the free ale and women I provide for you now I ask you to sacrifice yourself to my cause of conquering the world. Now in this day the church struggles to hold onto its people. Reformation is at hand and all is due to my master." The guard moves back slightly and continues to listen to his lord. "I will tell you that Satan himself divides the church, but the head of the church still remains. We must separate the head from the body. Killing the Pope would secure our victory. Heresy is not enough, it has proven so. Soon we will defeat Rome and God's instrument on earth, then we will rule and you by my side. I have seen you and you follow me like a dog follows a master. For this loyalty I will reward thee."

The guard smiles and his mind flows with images of glory, Magnus continues. "I will make you the second coming of a failed instrument of Satan. Your body will change into his image but your mind will remain. I will teach you what to say and eventually you will return to his followers and say you have returned to lead them. You see there was a German who stood against the instrument of God and he almost succeeded. I want him back and you will conquer in his name." The guard stands firm and says. "I am willing to do as you wish my lord." Magnus smiles deeply stepping away from the guard, lifting his hands to the sky palms upward. Mary lying on the cold wet ground watches the wizard while purple mist seeps from his hands, the colorful display surrounding the guard, the follower closing his eyes. Magnus moves his hands creating a whirlwind of mist around his follower. The wizard begins to speak his incantation. "Mist around may you bring back the Waldensian, give me my Peter Waldo." Slowly the guard begins to change, his image becoming one of an older gentleman with curly hair and a long beard. Suddenly the mist dissipates and the guard is now in the image of Peter Waldo an old heretic. Simon Magnus laughs with glee and says. "You are no longer a simple guard who drinks and fondles loose women. You are my Peter Waldo,\ defender of the Waldensians. You will bring back these beliefs to Italy and spout against the church.

The wizard laughs while the new Peter stands before him. Mary wide eyes and breathing heavy while her heart pounds with great fear. Magnus looks at his creation and says. "Now is your first day of study. You will be my protégé and follow my lead. You will learn all you can from me and eventually begin your deception upon the world. The guard who is now Peter Waldo smiles and bows to Simon Magnus, turning to the other guard who stands in fear, Peter says. "Now go and place that girl back on the horse. We move out with haste to the pass for our victory." Magnus smiles and realizes he has chosen wisely. The four figures mount their horses and continue towards Saint Bernard pass.

CHAPTER 10

The Confrontation

Bernard continued to ride throughout the night, the snow slightly falling upon the cold ground of the Turin province. Winters were harsh in Prali and the surrounding areas. Majority of folk tend to close their doors and shutters warming themselves with a cozy fire and soup in their belly. This night the priest finds himself searching for his friend Mary Archer. The lone traveler knew he would not reach his destination till the next day. He remembers the journey he had taken just over a year ago with Mary and a young knight named Leonardo. The memories of the journey run through his mind like sand in an hour glass. It seemed like yesterday he was on the search for the dragon that haunted the region and the victory he and Mary shared. Bernard knew he had an advantage over the sinister wizard. The vile villain carried a hostage while the priest carried nothing but his weapons and minor rations for the journey. If the monk rode hard through the night he would reach the pass before his foe. With the snow ever changing the ground cover he knew he could rely not on tracking but hope.

A short distance from the priest two figures shine in the night's sky, Tisiphone and Megaera flying overhead searching for the one who sent their sister back to the depths of hell. The image of the enemy fresh in the mind of Tisiphone, the image haunts the furia. The two sisters look for movement down below like hawks searching for its prey. Green trees, ponds, rivers, and mountains all in the sight of the furies. The pass of Saint Bernard seen in the distance. The cool wind blowing while the furies ride the winter sleet, in the distance Tisiphone uses her exceptional furia sight and locates the wizard with two others and a young girl tied to a horse. Suddenly she locates another traveling figure, a priest, and he is closing in on Magnus and his traveling party. Tisiphone connects the figures and realizes that the priest is on the hunt for her master, and the girl tied to the horse is the young English girl who was in her visions. The priest was the one the two furies searched for, now it was his time for him to die. Tisiphone looks over towards her sister Megaera and says. "The mortal we hunt is now below us. We must make a swift attack and send him to his God. It is only minutes till the priest catches up with the old wizard. We must not allow this to happen. It seems our master has done half the work for us by capturing the English girl. We will allow Magnus the thrill of the girl for now. Let's get this priest and make our revenge complete." Megaera nods her head with glee while both of the furies race to their target.

The holy priest can see the dark figures of the wizard and his two henchmen riding towards the pass while his companion is strapped to a horse. The priest was on the heels of the wizard when suddenly Bernard felt a painful surge rush through the left side of his body. His face hitting the cold ground of the forest, body numb from pain, swiftly he recovers his bearings realizing he has been attacked, his horse hiding in the trees just a few feet from the attack while the monk reaches for his sword within his sheath. The sword glistening in the moonlight, the priest ready to defend himself. Above him a familiar figure, a winged creature in the form of a female demon, a hell beast. The Franciscan remembered the creature he and his friend encountered before arriving to free Prali. The creature hovering above him, her wings flapping in the wind. The priest notices another demon creature similar to the one above him. Bernard was alone and prepared for the worst until his concentration broke with the sinister words the furia. "You priest will die! You defeated our sister

Alecto, but now you will die at the hands of her sisters." Bernard glared at the furies speaking above him and said. "If you two hell beasts are to battle a lone priests then give me the honor of knowing my enemy." Tisiphone continued to hover above and responded to the priests query. "My sister who you defeated her name was Alecto. My name is Tisiphone, and my sister beside you is Megaera." The priest gave a gentleman's nod of his head towards Megaera and with a wink of his eye launched himself toward Megaera.

Megaera moved from Bernard's reach, the priests sword missing his target. Megaera grabs her battle axe from her belt, the furia noticing that her weapon is not ablaze with fire. The battle axe useless against the priest, the power of fire was needed. Tisiphone notices this occurrence and shouts to her sister. "We are fools my sister! You have no power to attack this mortal. He has not committed the crime of infidelity and thus no power or responsibility of yours to fight him, your weapon is useless against him!" Tisiphone reaches for her whip and twirls it in the air, fire ignites from the whip, her weapon prepared for battle, Tisiphone instructs her sister. "Megaera the priest has committed murder and thus I can wreak vengeance upon him. Unless he commits infidelity you will have no power against him!" Megaera lowers her head to the ground in disappointment taking her battle axe in hand flying towards the air. Tisiphone speaks once more before engaging the priest. "Sister, watch the battle and if I am defeated you will go to the wizard and support his deeds at the pass." Megaera nods once more and watches the battle between her sister and the Franciscan. Alecto was the furia who castigated crimes of anger, she herself was the definition of pure anger. It was her job to cast anger against Bernard and Mary. Alecto never lost a fight until she encountered the two heroes. Tisiphone and Megaera never expected a loss and now only Tisiphone can battle the priest. Alecto the furia of anger and revenge for the crimes of anger and hate, Tisiphone the furia of murder and revenge for the crimes of murder. Megaera the furia of infidelity and the revenge for crimes against infidelity. Since Bernard committed no crime of infidelity, Megaera had no power to attack. Alecto attacked because she felt the anger in the hearts of Mary against Simon Magnus allowing her the opportunity to attack. Now that Bernard has the blood of Alecto on his hands Tisiphone can unleash her judgment upon him.

The furia with whip in hand engages the priest; the faith defender stands ready to defend himself against his enemy. The hellish creature twirls her whip and launches her projectile towards Bernard. The young priest seeing the attack ducks towards the ground, the whip slightly grazing the hair upon his head. The eager priest had to think of a path to victory, he had not his sword and his mortal sword had not much power over his enemy. The priest swings his sword towards the furia, The winged foe dodges his attack swinging her whip once more. The lashing weapon hitting its target wrapping itself around the priest's sword, the Franciscan holding on to his weapon with all his might, the whip tight around the sword while the creature pulls her weapon towards her. The evil dark fire surrounding her weapon overtaking the sword, she pulls her whip with aggression, the sword ripped from Bernard's hands landing a few feet behind Tisiphone. "You see priest, this is your destiny. Now I shall kill you on this earth and your soul will be sent to hell for my sisters and me to torment you for eternity." Bernard ignored the rant of the furia while he focuses on the sword, only the winged hell beast stood between him and his weapon. What can he do, his sword was no match for the weapons of a hell beast. He thought of how he could win over his enemy, and then he remembered. Mary dipped her arrows in holy water making her weapon a defender of God. The priest reached into his pocket and felt the cork of a bottle containing holy water. He loosened the cork with his finger, and once opened keeping his thumb over the bottle top. He needed to reach the sword and make it holy.

Tisiphone smiled knowing she had the priest in a vulnerable position, today was her victory. Until with a surprising move the faithful priest rushes towards her with all his strength within him. He knew it was a risk to rush toward the beast from oblivion, but he had little choice. Tisiphone tightening her grip upon the weapon with her hellish hands and raising her arms lifting the whip into attack position. Bernard was charging at full speed only seconds for the furia to react to this bold move. Tisiphone swings her whip towards her foe expecting the sound of the tip of the whip ripping the flesh from the benevolent priest. Bernard noticing the whip twirling towards him dives towards his sword doing a tuck and roll upon the ground. A move he had seen done in the past by Mary. It seemed his young friend has taught him well by her example from the time she dipped her arrows in holy water against the dragon to this moment. The whip from hell glided across the air missing the monk just slightly. The Vatican hero taking his sword in hand and with his opposite grasping the holy water from his pocket pouring it upon the sword making his weapon pure, a weapon heaven sent and blessed by heavenly powers of justice.

The furia turns and sees her opponent dousing the sword with water while her eyes grow with angry. Bernard rises from the ground, his sword soaked in holy water, and the priest's confidence peaked. Words between the two were not spoken only one thing ran through the minds of both hell beast and priest, "Victory." The roman priest now in a defensive position stands ready to prevail while the winged foe observes the stance of the enemy and calculating a proper attack. Once again the sinister dark creature raises her whip in hand and launches another attack. The Franciscan monk swiftly moving away from the attack until a sting against his cheek is felt upon his face while blood slowly travels down his cheek. The whip grazed him, the burning of the hell weapon searing through his head. The priest stunned at the attack notices the swiftness of his enemy, feeling the whip wrap around his waist. The winged servant of Satan with a multi attack upon the young Franciscan, her hands pulling the whip towards her with the Franciscan at the end of her weapon of evil, every step the priest takes is a step closer to destruction of his soul. "Come to me you little man." Tisiphone speaking to her victim in a sinister tone, her eyes red with anger and revenge while the priest still holds his sword in hand, the furia pulls him closer into her, the fire burning through the priest's religious habit and creating pain upon his delicate skin. "Come to me, come to me to die." her laughter increases with each step being forced upon Bernard. The fire of the whip begins to burn the clothes of the Franciscan even more so while his cheek burned with the feeling of fire. "This is just a taste my foe, soon you will be consumed by the fires of hell." Tisiphone continued to taunt, but the priest did not dare to attempt to take his hand and pull on the whip for fear his hand would be consumed by the fire, though his clothes became more of the victim of the whip. The devilish creature now pulling the monk just a few feet from her position, she wanted to breathe into his face to let him know he was defeated.

Bernard held his sword in hand, Tisiphone dragging him towards her. The Franciscan now only a step away from the furia while the fire began to take hold of his clothes, soon he would be consumed by the fires of hell and his immortal body ripped asunder. The winged beast pushing Bernard to the ground, her wings flapping faster with excitement of victory as the fire around her foe grows and grows with increasing speed. Now she wanted to take her hands and wrap it around his neck. She wanted to dig her nails into his flesh and spread her inner fire into his mortal veins. Tisiphone reaches to strike him until a fire is felt through her own body. Looking down towards her left side she notices the sword of the Franciscan within her. The feeling was not that of an ordinary sword but that of a heavenly weapon. The holy water had done its job and worked on the furia. Slowly the furia's fingers turn to ash, her arms, and soon the rest of her while she screams in tormented pain and disbelief of her demise. A swift wind picks up and blows the ashes of her body into the wind, the priest lying upon the ground while the whip around his waist becomes dust. Rising from the ground he performs the sign of the cross upon his chest and placing his sword within his sheath. The priest realized that the furia had delayed him to face Simon Magnus, but maybe that was the plan of the wizard all along. The Vatican loyalist hoped and prayed that Mary was ok for now and worried for her wellbeing. He looked up towards the pass of Saint Bernard and said. "Now time to face the wizard once and for all."

Simon Magnus and his men reached the pass looking for the opening of the cavernous dwelling that once held him. He turns to his captive who is strapped to a horse and says. "Look girl, do you remember this place? It is the pass where you defeated the dragon and freed me from my prison. Now I will make this your tomb and my victory against the world." With his mighty power he lifted the rocks from the ground creating an opening into the cave. The pass was now open once more while Simon and his men enter with Mary defeated and fit to be tied. The church within the pass changed since the battle with the dragon. The center of the floor was now a large hole that seemed to lead to the center of the earth. Magnus turned to the poor innocent girl tied to the horse and said. "The hole you created dear girl is the tomb of the dragon. He fell down into this massive hole, the abyss. It is the entry way into hades itself. From this hole I will cast my spells and forge an army of hellish beasts. Nothing will be able to defeat them, nothing at all. In fact I have furia watching the skies now as we speak. They work for me, and they do my bidding." Mary thought of his words and realized who the furia were and the battle of one on the road before Prali. Peter Waldo approached Magnus and said. "My lord I wonder where the furia are now. We have not seen them in many days now." Magnus glares at his follower and answers. "Furia do what needs to be done. They know my needs and work behind the scenes of my victory. Have no fear Waldo; they will come to me when I summon their fellow brothers and sisters from the gates of hell."

Not far off in the distance from the wizard of darkness a lone Franciscan priest rides into the unknown evening of the Turin Province. One thing is on the mind of this priest and one thing only. To defeat the evil grip held by the wizard and to save his friend from the inevitable demise. He rides fast in the darkness to bring light into the world. Bernard was coming for Magnus and his minions.

CHAPTER 11

Saint Bernard's Pass

The lone furia Megaera flies down to a perched location above the cavernous grounds of the pass. Her position can observe all within the large cave dwelling that once acted as a church in the time of Saint Bernard. Thought to be forgotten but rediscovered by Mary Archer and Bernard while tracking the dragon who attacked the town of Prali and the surrounding areas, the same location that imprisoned Simon Magnus and now the final day of the innocent English girl Mary Archer. The last of the furia observes the wizard and his men entering the large cave while the girl remains tied to the horse, her feet and hands still bound. Simon Magnus looks around the cave and sees the old altar in the distance. "Move the girl to the altar. We will let her lay there till it is time to perform the ritual of final victory over this world and the followers of the church." Magnus commanding his men and instructing them while Peter helps carry the girl to the altar and eventually once his task is completed moves to stand by his master and dreams of the day he may be leader of the new world order. "What shall we do for now?" Peter asking his master a basic question, Magnus responds. "I will prepare to have the girl sacrificed and you shall think of a clever way to show yourself to the world once we have completed our task here. You will use the Waldensian to control the region and with me forcing Rome to her knees. Together we will control all things and I will be the new god of this world. I will give you Italy and its entire people. You will do with them as you will." Peter smiled ear to ear after listening to the wizard and his plan for world domination.

Bernard riding as fast as his steed can carry him stopping for nothing, he felt the urgency to ride without hesitation or fear. Riding towards the entry of Saint Bernard's Pass he remembered it well and could never forget the events that took place sometime ago. The entry way in clear view the priest notices the removal of rock and debris; he knew it was the work of the first heretic. The night became cold while the stars faded behind the incoming clouds above. In the distance bats could be heard and a brisk air swirled around the entry. The Vatican priest leaped from his horse and used rope to tie his steed to a large boulder, gripping his sword he moved towards the dim light shining from the entry. The Franciscan crossed his chest with the sign of the cross whispering a prayer to remind himself of his heavenly faith looking back towards his horse and the darkness of night. He wondered who would replace him if he failed this night. The Church had armies but would they withstand the ancient wizard, the first wizard of this world. Slowly Bernard moves within the entry while the evil voice of the wizard echoes in the distance, no sound coming from his friend who was bound and gagged. His right hand remained rested on the hilt of his sword, hand damp with sweaty nervousness, his heart pounding with excitement. Reminiscent of the time he fought the dragon. Shadows from the light within the cave became into focus seeing the evil magician and his men. The priest now standing in the entryway of the large room within the mountain pass observing the wizard preparing for spells of wizardry while in a corner a man unknown to Bernard is kneeling in some type of prayer or deep thought, behind the altar was one of the guards of Magnus, and upon the altar was Mary Archer. The Franciscan flinched once he noticed his friend but did not dare make himself known at this time. Megaera noticed Bernard but said nothing to warn the evil leader.

Suddenly Peter Waldo lifts his head and notices a lone figure in the entry. Turning to Magnus he yells, "My lord we have a visitor before us." Lifting off the ground and standing with his hand placed against the dagger secured in his belt. Simon Magnus turns swiftly and sees Bernard in the doorway. Mary who lay upon the altar smiles under the handkerchief upon her mouth, her sweat loosening the rope binding her hands. The delusional wizard begins to walk towards the Vatican priest but stops short and says. "Welcome my Franciscan, now you will know the meaning of pain. I have to admit I learned much from my first master Dositheus and also being expelled by the apostles. Justin who by Church eyes in now a saint disliked my methods, and then there was the battle with the so-called Saint Bernard who encased me in ice for many years. Now you stand before me at the dawn of the new and advanced Simonians, my followers. You see young priest I have lived for over a thousand years. Granted it has been the majority of time in ice, but now is my time. I am the new god for the new age of man." Bernard placed his hand on his hilt, Magnus noticing his move and said. "Ta-ta priest, you forget that I have the sword of Peter. Your sword has nothing it can offer in battle." Simon Magnus reveals the sword of great power from behind his back; he raises the sword and points it towards the priest continuing to speak. "You see lowly coward this is only a start of the great work and wonders I shall perform. Soon ArAm Raad will bring me back the shroud of Turin and the spear that was thrust into the side Jesus while he hung from the cross. The more relics I combine the more power I shall hold, until one day I shall rule all and your people will be my footstool."

Bernard feared for the sword of Peter until he realized that the sword was holy and pure. The words of the wizard were a blur to the priest. He cared not for the plans of evil; his concentration was on the rescue of Mary and defeating evil. When he heard the name of the infidel ArAm Raad his ears perked up and he answered the fiendish foe. "I have bad news for you wizard, your leader, ArAm Raad. He is dead." The eyes of the purple gowned wizard grew angry while Bernard continued. "You see he returned to Prali after a battle of some kind. I can tell you that his company shown blood stains on their armor and their numbers few, a true sign of defeat. When your troops entered Prali the town's people killed your men including this infidel ArAm Raad. His body was torn to pieces and burned to nothingness just like his faith and the faith you have in yourself. This may surprise you and you may not even know this, but when you leave your power and influence leaves with you. You cannot hold your power over people unless your presence is there. That is your weakness wizard and it has always been so." Bernard steps towards Magnus and into the light making himself visible to all within the dwelling.

Magnus did his best not to show frustration at the news the priest brought with him, and the wizard responds. "You sir may speak truth but with the relics I can hold the power and hold it indefinite." Lifting his sword he offers the priest a challenge. "Come Franciscan and embrace me in battle. Now I shall send you to your maker." With the words of his master Peter Waldo runs towards Bernard with dagger in hand, the guard also charges the priest from behind the altar. Mary seeing the action turns her body towards one of the corners of the altar placing her hands upon it and moving her hands up and down, the rope rubbing against the corner of the altar. The guard and Peter advanced simultaneously towards Bernard, the guard coming from the right and Waldo to the left. Both men coming at such a great rate of speed with weapons in hand they came ever closer until at the last second Bernard stepped forward causing both men to collide, there speed not able to stop in time. The guard and Peter slam each other to the ground; just moans are heard from the floor by both men behind Bernard. The priest looks down at the men and snickers, then turns to Simon Magnus and says. "Is this the best you got wizard? These men are nothing in the realm of battle." The wizard glares towards his foe while his lips curl into an evil grin listening to the Franciscans arrogance, responding. "They are not meant for fighting, Peter is a tool to advance my agenda and the guard I have no excuse for. Nevertheless you shall die by my hand not theirs." Bernard takes his sword from its sheath and turns to Peter Waldo. "Magnus you are right about one thing." Bernard raising his sword against Waldo and thrusting it into his chest as the sound of penetration echoes throughout the cavernous chamber. Peter Waldo stunned by the defeat begins to shake in agony his blood curdling scream echoing throughout the cavern. "This man Magnus I will not die by his hands for sure." Bernard finishing the statement made before killing Peter Waldo. The devilish wizard now furious at Bernard for slaying Peter Waldo, his hands clinching, wanting to strike the priest with his bare fists. "Magnus I guess there goes your plan for the Waldensians to take the Turin region and Prali." The guard stumbles to his feet and regains his composure, lifting his sword to battle Bernard.

The guard swings his sword towards Bernard only to be met by steel. The Franciscan and the guard in mortal combat while Mary Archer continues to rub the rope against the altar corner hoping to escape her predicament and help her friend who is in the heat of battle. Simon Magnus begins to chant a spell from his lips, his eyes begin to glow red as blood as a purple mist surrounds him. The priest and the guard exchanging blow for blow, the swords clashing, echoing through the caverns and out into the cold mountain air. Mary continuing to set herself free, until suddenly she had done what she set out to do, the girl was free. She leans in toward her feet and unties the rope binding her feet together and finally the handkerchief in her mouth removed. The archer observes the room looking for her weapons with frustration and urgency. Finally noticing her weapons dangling from the late Peter Waldo's horse, the young girl doing her best not to be noticed by the menacing wizard conjuring spells of evil magic and the guard who is in a death battle with her priestly friend while she creeps slowly towards the recovery of her items of battle, she reaches her destination slowly placing her arrows in the proper place. Simon Magnus begins to levitate from the floor while his body is surrounded by purple mist, daggers form from his finger nails pointing in the direction of Bernard. Swords clash in the night, both Bernard and the guard exchanging blows. Suddenly an arrow enters the temple of the guard's head, blood exploding in all directions. The guard slowly falls to the ground, the arrow shooting out from the other end of his head. The blood soaking the face of the priest as the blood splatters in all directions. The hero in the habit turns to the direction of the arrows origins and he sees a familiar image and the sound of her voice reigns true. "Enough play time friend, let's end this once and for all." The facial expression on the face of Mary was one of revenge for her friends and the town of Prali.

The wizard realizes the girl set herself free and that his guard failed him once more. He steps back to keep both the girl and the priest in his line of sight, then he speaks to Mary in a sinister voice. "Young lady, you think you are safe but you are not. So Peter Waldo is dead and the head of my guard has been turned into Swiss cheese. This does not stop my domination; it just means I have new men to find to help in my conquest." His evil stare penetrates the girl's soul, pointing his hands towards her. Without hesitation the daggers from his hands take flight towards Mary. The speed of travel is swift while the archer girl does her best to avoid the wizards attack. She ducks down toward the ground and a sharp pain strikes her right shoulder. Taking her left hand and placing it on the hurt wound, she feels blood and the dagger that made its mark. She knew luck was on her side, only one hit out of ten, the other nine daggers hit and implanting deep within the rocked wall. The purple mist continues to build around Magnus. He is now almost impossible to see as the fearless priest charges the wizard without a sound except for his footsteps. He raises his sword high above his head to strike the levitating wizard; Magnus lifts himself higher above the ground. Bernard runs into the mist to only find himself on the other side of the room. He missed the wizard completely. Mary lifts herself from the ground, leaning against the wall for support. She notices the wizard floating upon the purple mist with the sword of Saint Peter in his hands.

The young archer takes an arrow from her sheath and places it in her crossbow, the pain of her shoulder making it difficult to pull the arrow back. She pants while the blood runs from her shoulder and down her side remembering what her father taught her about aim and precision. Her body begins to shake while focusing on the aim to strike the wizard. Sweat beads down her face, finally the arrow launches, only to miss the wizard completely. She tries another attack and misses again. The notorious wizard notices her injury and the effort she is making to attack. He laughs and speaks in a taunting voice. "My girl you are weak and the dagger runs deep within your shoulder. You have no aim and I am getting bored with you. I transformed Skulk into Decorus to make something ugly into something beautiful. Now I shall turn something innocent and beautiful into something wretched and ugly." He laughs while the mist continues to support him in defense. Suddenly a black mist forms only around his hands. "You my lady will become the most horrid creature alive." Magnus continues to taunt while the girl loads another arrow, her glare focusing on the wizard while she desperately tries to places another arrow in the crossbow. The black mist coming closer to her as her heart pounds and she breathes gasping in freight. The mist that will transform her into a creature of ill repute slithers towards her like a snake in the grass. Suddenly Simon Magnus screams in agony while he falls from his perched position upon the purple mist. Bernard taking his sword in hand jumped up towards the wizard and sinks his weapon into the enemy's foot.

The Vatican priest and the wizard possessed face each other in the mist; Magnus raises his sword towards Bernard to battle once and for all. The black mist continues towards Mary while she slowly moves away using the wall to balance herself. Simon Magnus looks deep into the eyes of his enemy and says. "Today you will die by the sword of the apostle and my victory will be complete." The sly wizard moves his hands forward to strike the monk but nothing happens, it is like his arm has no strength or as if the priest had a shield around him. The sword of Saint Peter begins to shake making Magnus tremble, the sword bringing the wizard to his knees. The hands of the evil one becoming numb from the shaking, the wizard loosens his grip from the sword and moves back from the heavenly power of steel and might. Bernard looks at Magnus and says. "You see wizard! Evil cannot harness something that is good. Only one who follows the one true God can wield the sword of Saint Peter. The evil magician continues to move backwards closer to the giant hole in the middle of the cave flooring. Magnus realizing that he is too close to the edge moves forward to keep a distance from the hole, and then speaks to Bernard. "You may have the sword but you see the opening in the ground? That my friend is one of the seven gates of hell. The hole leads to the center of the earth where Satan resides. Before I made myself known to the world I conjured a spell and summoned the gate to open allowing me powers to request the help of the furia. I will kill you and you friend, sending you to hades through this passage."

Bernard runs towards the sword of Peter and places it in his sheath. Once more the sword is with him and the priest knows that nothing evil can hold the sword. Simon Magnus speaks in tongues, his words unintelligible, and his eyes becoming red as blood. "This night you will be sent to hell and the demons will feed on your soul for all eternity." With those words the wizard launches another attack, a red beam from each eye. Bernard cannot believe what he is witnessing but he cannot think of such things, his only thought is to defend himself from attack. The beams come towards him while he swings his sword against the attack. His sword blocks the beam attack of death while he notices the black mist slowly coming towards the injured Mary Archer. The wizard now begins to taunt Bernard as well as the girl. "You see priest, soon your little friend will become something so sick that you will not even lay eyes on her. I will change her and with her hate of herself she throw herself into the gate of hell, it's inevitable." With those words Magnus forms another attack of his beams, Bernard taking another swing and evading the attack. Mary on the floor moving her body back away from the black mist as best as she can, taking a small vile of holy water and throws it against the oncoming mist. Nothing works for the girl while the mist continues to come closer to her.

The priest continuing to keep his defensive stance while thinking of a way to save his dear friend from the creeping mist of transformation and unspeakable horrors of this world, slowly the mist approaches the victim. Simon Magnus continuing to block Bernard from assisting Mary using his beams. From Behind the priest the sound horse hooves, several of them, until a gust of wind knocked him to the floor. The priest landing face first upon the floor disoriented from the surprise attack. "Was it another attack by Magnus?" He thought to himself. A second later his question to himself was answered. One hundred French soldiers charged Simon Magnus on horseback, his beams shooting from his eyes without mercy. Soldier after soldier falling from their horses like dominoes while the beams hit their chests and penetrated their armor, the beams causing shock and electrifying the armor of the French while screams from the mouths of men and burnt flesh begin to rise to the ceiling of the cavern. Simon Magnus laughs while he kills each soldier, though he didn't realize how many Frenchmen were charging forward. His purple mist becoming a hindrance to his own vision, until suddenly a wall of French knights came towards him, his beams not enough to stop all of them. The horses knocking the delusional wizard to the ground, his purple and black robe catching onto one of the horses saddle buckles. The French knights not noticing the large hole beyond the mist ride straight to their doom and into the gate of hades. Simon Magnus trying to unlatch himself still caught onto the buckle falls with the Frenchmen on horseback. The screams of the men and Magnus being heard throughout the mountain pass until their voices became suddenly silent. The black mist surrounding Mary dissipates just before it turns her into something unnatural, a sign of the death of Magnus. The power of the wizard is no more and the damage he had done to the people of Prali and the region has come to an end. His mist of purple and black dissipate in the air of night.

Standing before Bernard was a young Frenchman, he greets the priest. "Hello father, it is a pleasure to meet you. My name is Clement Laurent." The priest placing himself at ease extends his hand to Clement and says. "Thank you for coming, you save us just in time. Things were about to get ugly. How did you know about us and where we were?" Clement Laurent smiled with a look of confidence and said in response. "After we defeated the Persians at Briancon we buried their dead and then followed their tracks to Prali. We thought it unwise for a French troop to enter Italy, but under the circumstances we thought it proper. We thought the Pope would not mind since France and Italy both serves him with honor. After hearing from the people about the story of the wizard and the priest we thought we would lend a hand and finish the journey." Bernard thanked Clement once more while French soldiers helped Mary to her feet and tended to her wound. The holy priest looking over the shoulder of Clement said. "Will Mary be ok?" Clement smiled and responded. "Have no worries father my men will take good care of her." The men carried Mary to the Franciscan and placed her before him. The two friends embraced, tears formed in their eyes while they knew they escaped another close call against evil. Their embrace continues while Bernard comforts his friend saying. "I will see you at the bottom of the mountain pass," the young girl shaking her head in agreement.

The priest, English girl, and the French soldiers leave the cavern for the bottom of the mountain. Watching everything from above the lone furia Megaera who felt the sting of defeat as her blood flowed with envy and anger. In her cold heart she feels jealousy over what she had seen. Jealous over the friendship of Mary and Bernard and the support of the French troops who saved the day for the two friends, the furia realizing her existence was nothing more than a lie. She was created from evil and sin. Her mission in life was to judge those who were jealous; she was the soldier of the green eye of jealousy. For the first time she felt jealousy in her own heart, a crime in her eyes. Megaera knew the only way into the gates of hell was to die again. Hell would not let her in without sacrifice. Once Magnus freed her from hell to do his bidding her only way back was to die. She did not think of such a thing since she was sure Simon Magnus would be victorious. Megaera lifts herself from her propped position and floats down to the edge of the hole in the floor, the entrance to hell. Reaching for a dagger in her pouch, she takes it in hand, placing it to her heart, thrusting it into her chest. A tear runs down her cheeks as she says. "I can see you my sisters, I will be home soon." Her limp body falling into the hole, and finally reaching the final destination and once again together with her sisters of evil and hate, the only life the poor furia will ever know.

CHAPTER 12

Magic and Miracles

The French stitched up Mary the best they could under the circumstances, thankfully for her they were prepared for war and brought medicine men. The English girl thanked all involved in her care and noticed Clement Laurent standing with a horse, his grip holding tight the reins. She walks towards him and gives him an innocent smile. Clement returns the greeting and says in his deep French accent. "My lady you bring me a beautiful innocent smile, but I think you are not innocent in the ways of the world." She did not know what to think of his words, a slight chuckle leaving her sensual lips. "My good sir I admit in a situation regarding dragons and wizards, death, misfortune, I am no stranger to such things, though in regards to other things I am completely innocent." Clement gave an understanding laugh and moved his hand holding the reins towards Mary. "Here my lady this horse is for your journey back to Prali. My men and I must take another route. We don't want to be detected past the Turin region. If you ever find your way to France please come and visit us sometime. We would be delighted to be in your presence. You may come and visit my homestead in Orleans." Mary thankful for the invitation responded. "Thank you Clement, maybe someday. I do admit though that I miss my home land of Lancashire. My family once lived in Haslingden and I wish to return some day." She moved her hand and taking the reins from Clement, their hands touching, she felt something within her, and she was charmed by the Frenchman.

She hoisted herself upon the horse, her shoulder bandaged and prepared for the journey home. Bernard said his thankful farewells to the French soldiers and promised Clement Laurent that he would inform the Pope of the tremendous deeds of his troops and his valiant leadership. The priest turns to his friend, their horse facing North West. "Well my dear Mary should we travel back to the road leading into Prali?" She laughs and remembers the journey back to Prali after defeating the dragon. "Yes father I am ready to do so but first let me ask you a question." Bernard sat up straight upon his horse and perked his ears, she continued with a curious query. "What is the difference between the magic performed by Simon Magnus and what the saints perform? Would you say it is all magic?" Bernard looked at her with a sincere smile and said. "The difference between magic and miracles is this. Miracles are from heaven, magic is from hell. You see God supplies those who serve him with miracles, and miracles show and bring people closer to God. Magic on the other hand is from Satan and shows people how to move away from God. Simon Magnus in the beginning followed the apostles until he became jealous, he wanted power, fame, and fortune. He was doing it for himself. The apostles did it for God, to show Gods love. Anyone who tells you they can do magic or performs magic is working for the underworld. Our world is a constant battle of good versus evil, miracles versus magic. Any wizard, even if they say they are good, is actually from Satan. Be wary of magic Mary, for all the history of the world people will perform magic and miracles. It is the saints versus the wizards, there is no such thing as a good wizard. The closest thing to a good wizard is a saint, and saints work for God. The battle between the two will continue till the second coming and in my soul I feel that a bigger battle will soon be here. Simon Magnus spoke of the large opening in the pass as a gateway to hell. If this is the case then we have to be vigilante of evil."

Mary listened to the words of Bernard and said. "I hope it never happens, I am tired of evil. We have fought a dragon and a wizard in a two year span. Do you think it is the hole causing this? Both dragon and wizard came from the same location. Maybe the pass itself is evil. Should we block the hole somehow?" The priest looked forward and responded. "My girl it is not up to us, we have done our share. It is up to men like Clement Laurent and others to defend the world. You are just a girl, and I a priest. I'm not sure if the hole conjured the dragon or Magnus, all I know is that evil exists and we must defend against it. Clement knows of the dangers ahead and when he returns to France he will supply his people and the surrounding countries information about the Persians and their entry into Europe with the help of Simon Magnus. Europe should be warned to never surrender their country or culture to the invaders of the east. It is up to the people of Europe to cultivate their faith and culture. If not, evil will prevail in the image of magic or the image of the east. This should be remembered for all times. We live in a dangerous time Mary. Popes speak of crusades and Germans speak of reforms. We must stay the course and defend what's ours." Mary looked at the kind hearted priest as if she had been filled with astonishing words, and then she regained herself and said. "You have come so far Bernard and I am happy to know you. Now you have spoken of a course. I say let's get on that course and go home to Prali." The two friends smile while they gallop towards the west.

On the road back to Prali the two friends spoke of their adventure against the dragon and the battle against Simon Magnus. The scenery they pass on the road home reminded them of the adventures and the times they had. Winter was upon them but they knew that soon spring would be here and a new day will dawn. Finally the fork in the road, one road leading into Prali and the other back to Rome where the monk must make his journey and the archer back to her small little house in the small little town on the opposite road. There was a third road and it brought back memories of his time in the Franciscan monastery in Prali. Turning to his friend the faithful priest speaks. "You think any of my brothers still reside there?"

Mary laughs and responds. "Do you miss your old life as a monk? I think you look grand as a priest. I am sure maybe one or two of your brothers are there but you know how it is in religious life, moving from one country to another." Bernard laughed and knew his friend was right. "Yes Mary you are learning all there is about monastic life but a monk will always be a monk no matter how far they elevate up the chain of church command. Maybe one day it shall call you." She ponders her friend's words and nodded slightly. The two friends embraced upon their horses and said their farewells. Both of them knew that they would see each other again someday. Bernard trots south towards Rome, while Mary takes the short road to Prali.

The clouds moved through the sky, the sun slightly peering through. She looked around her while she came close to Prali. The farms were back to normal and all was at peace with the world. Entering Prali the people acted as though nothing had happened, even a new priest resided in the church. It seems the people moved swiftly after the last battle in Prali. Finally she found herself back on her homestead and then she thought of her mother. How she missed her mother and longed for a greeting at the door. Riding her horse into the stable she thought of the work and cleaning that needed to be done. How the invasion of her home infuriated her, though she had the last word. Walking to her front door she noticed it was ajar. She entered the home and found her friend Annalisa standing before her with a dish and towel in hand. Mary sprang into action and embraced her friend while the crashing sound of the plate hitting the floor is heard. The two girls hold each other for some time, until Mary decides to speak and move from their embrace. "Tell me what happened and what happened to you?" Annalisa still in mourning over her fiancé answers the query. "Once the French arrived they located me and rescued me. The entire city liberated and eventually I could not find you, so I came here. Once I realized you were gone I decided to clean your place and prayed for your return. I knew not what happened to you but I never gave up hope."

Mary was happy her friend survived the invasion of Magnus, and responded. "Never give up hope Annalisa. Where there is evil there is always good. To find good in all of us and keep it close to our hearts. In time good always conquers evil, even if at times it seems impossible." Annalisa smirked and said. "Mary you have really learned something, where did you go, Rome?" Mary laughed and said. "No my friend I was in the mountain pass and with much worry, but that is a different matter altogether and I dare not share the adventure with you now. Let's rest and have a cozy supper by the fire." An hour passed and the two friends enjoyed a pleasant meal together and then Mary asked her friend a question that surprised even her. "You know I am all alone here and nobody to share life with. I know with your loss you are feeling alone as well as I am with the loss of my mother. Annalisa . . . " She pauses and then continued, holding back her emotions. "Would you like to live here in my home with me?" Annalisa smiles with happiness in her soul and says. "I would like that very much Mary." both girls laugh and their night filled with firelight and friendship.

Bernard spent many nights on the road traveling back to Rome. Once he returned he unpacked his belongings and made some tea for himself. He thought of what had transpired and knew the Pope would want a full report of what had taken place. Suddenly a knock came to his door, getting up from his chair he opens the door to find a young monk. The monk was a mere boy, probably a first year novice. "Are you Bernard the priest who arrived from the Turin region?" The Priest didn't realize anyone noticed him enter his abode, responding to the young monk. "Yes lad I am he, what may I do for you?" The monk responds to Bernard with a deep nervous breath. "His Holiness wants to see you now." The obedient priest rolls his eyes and realizes he is tired from his journey and says. "I don't want to sound rude but can this wait till tomorrow? I will have a full report for the Pope in the morn." The monk responds. "No sir, His Holiness wants to see you right away." Without hesitation Bernard retrieves his coat and makes his way to Saint Peter's Basilica. Moments pass while Bernard sat in a waiting room waiting to be seen. His eyes began to feel heavy and slumber almost captured him until a nudge from a Cardinal woke him. "The Pope will see you now Father Bernard."

The meeting with the Pope went through the night and in the end Bernard was left with only his duty to perform for the church. The Pope ordered Bernard to return the sword to the church for safe keeping; they did not want the sword to fall in the wrong hands, though the sword is useless to evil men. The church wanted to protect the sword for historical reasons, like the shroud of Turin and other artifacts that belonged to the church. Bernard knew that someday the sword would rise again to fight evil and in the end be victorious. Walking slowly to his residence he placed his hand upon the doorknob and turned it slowly. Walking into his place of rest and relaxation he threw off the coat and fell upon his bed, at this moment the sun began to break over the mountain and valleys of Italy. There in an undisclosed home Bernard slept and dreamed like he had never dreamed before. The smile upon his face was proof of his pleasant slumber. Rome, Prali, and the world were once more at peace. It is true that the crusaders marched on against evil, but for the rest of the world peace was at hand and a new day dawned, a time of peace and tranquility for the human race with a bright future ahead.

Short Stories through Adventures

By Davidson L. Haworth

A Short Forward

Most of my life I have been writing in some form or another, but never thought of the short story. In my youth I enjoyed a good story here and there but never thought of writing one until I traveled to the Russian Federation in 2010. Walking the streets of Moscow a person can get the feel of why the society in Russia is a literary culture. Russia has produced some of the greatest writers. For example, Alexander Pushkin, Ivan Bunin, Anton Chekhov, Leo Tolstoy, just to name a few. Being surrounded by the same locations and streets these literary legends walked it is easy to get influenced to write something from the heart. One cure for writers block is to travel to Russia and experience it. This is where "The Mighty Babushka" my short story is created and written. Being raised in San Jose, California a person is far removed from Russia, especially growing up in the 1980's, but there was one Russian who influenced me. His name was Pyotr Ilyich Tchaikovsky, the man who wrote many compositions including "The Nutcracker." Every year my father would take me to the San Jose Performing Arts Center and experience the live performance of this amazing ballet.

Most of my life the music of Tchaikovsky has been with me, from a small child, till this very day. All my life I wanted to see the piano Tchaikovsky used to write this masterpiece and in 2010 I traveled from Moscow to the town of Klin to fulfill that dream. Klin is the location of Tchaikovsky's home and where he wrote "The Nutcracker." Seeing, touching, and walking in the home of the great composer and seeing the actual piano, it inspired me to write, and in the back of Tchaikovsky's home sitting on a bench surrounded by snow I wrote the short story "The Might Babushka." The March weather in Klin was kind to me and so were the people of that fine little town. It will always remain in my heart.

Russia is also the inspiration for "The Eye of Devastation" a short story written because of one lonely young girl standing in a Moscow metro station with a sign reading "Please give me money so I can have a new eye." The girl stood there in tattered clothes with only one eye and not even a patch to cover the exposed destroyed eye. It moved me almost to tears as I thought of her life and the misery she must be suffering.

The short story "Your Time Will Come" is a short two paragraph story about a foreign exchange student. In 2010 two German tourists were killed on the streets of San Francisco and I thought of the brutal streets of that dilapidated city, and I thought of the fear those two German victims must have felt in the hands of evil criminals. This incident inspired me to write a little something to remind me of those victims because no victim should ever be forgotten. Another victim of another sort is the California Grizzly and my short story "The Last Grizzly" tries to capture the life and times of two girls living in California and their experiences with a hunter. Hope you enjoy these experiences through fiction.

The Mighty Babushka

By Davidson L. Haworth

The year, 1882 A.D., the sun beamed down upon the home surrounded with snow and ice. The morning sky clear, the flake of snow falling from the large trees, winter was making its exit and spring slowly arriving. March being a time of change in the small town of Klin and people began to shed their winter coats for the bright sunshine. Sitting upon my chair turning towards the window, observing the change, the sun peering through the window, the beams touching my face, feeling like a warm kiss upon my cheeks, there was only one kiss I needed, the tender kiss of my love.

Down below on the street a loud noise was heard. Standing from my chair I walked towards the window, the glaring sun upon my face. I noticed an elderly woman tapping the rears of the school children walking past her on the street corner. The elderly woman's words stern and spoken with authority. "Move along children, move along." She muttered. It was a cool but sunny afternoon, the children walking home from school. Observing the children I noticed they were walking over black ice. Black ice is frequent this time of year, months of snow now giving way to the coming of spring.

The elderly woman well known in the community, she is the protector of her neighbors. She is a Babushka, a woman with no family. Her husband died at age fifty-four. The Babushka was only forty at the time of her loves death. With no children, the Babushka adopted the people of her community.

Today the children being policed by her, the Babushka knows children don't think of the slippery hard ice under their feet. The people of Klin, including the children are anxious for the arrival of spring. Klin experiences six to seven months of snow. March is the most dangerous of times. It's not difficult to hear stories of people breaking legs or ankles. The children pass the Babushka, who watches and protects. The old woman looks onward, praying the children will be safe on the remainder of their homeward journey. Making the sign of the cross three times in her Orthodox fashion she moves on looking for others to guide.

A young farmer in his mid-twenties, his hair balding, face marred by his stressful experiences in life. His clothes dirty and worn from his daily work, there is never a day of rest for Demetri Kuysnich. All of his life was spent avoiding the Babushka, he feared her. Demetri inherited his farm land from his dying father at the age of sixteen. His mother died during child birth. His father so loved his mother, another wife was never taken for his father. Demetri has been alone since his father's death. Others his age would spend time drinking vodka and picking up on the local ladies of Klin in the town center. One day he hoped for a wife, but his duties prevented such dreams. A farmer with no hope except for the hope of fresh morning milk and eggs from his own animals, and what crops can he produce with such rubbish weather and soil.

For myself I am just an average citizen of Klin. My two story home surrounded by windows, North, south, east, west. Imported English drapes surround the large windows, allowing the sun to peer through. Though I am Russian, pleasant drapes and a good spot of tea suits me fine. Perched from my second story home I can observe my fellow citizens of Klin. The north side of my home overlooks the town center from a distance. My view allows me to peek at the male drunkards. The west side of my home observes the farm of Demitre, just half mile away. In all directions I watch the babushka daily, at times hourly. I have never met the Babushka, Demitre, or the drunks personally. I rarely leave my home; I am a writer and only living on my published words.

My servant is of Mongolian decent, given to me by a rich widow who enjoys my works. In fact the home I live in is not mine; it belongs to the elderly rich widow who supplies me with my needs. This luxurious home became my prison over the years writing for a woman who loves to publish my works, and reads my stories to her spoiled grandchildren.

This morning is like any other morning. Wake up at the crack of dawn, walk down to the cold kitchen, never walking barefoot. The wood within the fireplace, always taking time to heat up the home, my Mongolian servant, whose name I can never pronounce wakes up two hours before the break of dawn heating the rooms with kerosene lamps and warm fires. I sipped my tea watching the babushka with the children. To my north the drunks begin to gather in the town center, still hung over from the night before. Then there is Demitre who is awake before all of Klin. The rest of my day spent writing and the urge to sleep. The quills to paper making my eyes feel the sting of an afternoon nap. Watching the Babushka in the morning and now in the afternoon, smiling while she watched over the children, her work never done to improve her community from the drags of society and the people who cannot look after themselves, especially those children who have to fend for themselves between walking from home to school and back again.

The next day I heard the voice of the Babushka from within my home, her voice carried from the withered winter outside, loud and thunderous her tone. Where did it originate this time? From the town center the Babushka defends a young attractive girl from the drunks, her cane knocking the knees of one of the drunks. "How dare you touch this young lady in such a manner?" The Babushka chiding the drunk while the other drunkards watch with amusement.

The Babushka had been sitting in the town center observing the drunks while a young innocent girl around the age of fourteen walking through the town center on her way home from visiting a friend, the four drunks whistling and calling to the young girl, including one drunk who shouted. "Come to me girl, sit on my lap!" The drunks doing what most men do. Take advantage of innocent girls for their own selfish lusts. The Babushka and I agreed on one thing. Men are arrogant, selfish beings, Gods worse creation. How many girls have fallen victim to the stalkers of the night? In Klin I can honestly say several. These drunk or non-drunk bastards think of women as tools and toys for the male gender. How ignorant are the women? They always fall for the lies of men.

This time the young girl was smart, ignoring the advances of the drunken men. The Babushka came to the rescue, my eyes watered thinking of all the girls who fall prey to these men. Witnessing such vulgarity on the weekend nights, the men of Klin lived like kings. Their women worked while they drank the day away. Vodka bottles littered the town center and most of Klin. Drinking their vodka and returning in the evening. Slapping their wives around or sexually abusing them.

Today the fourteen year old girl with soft porcelain skin, blue eyes, and golden hair, she successfully escaped the drunks, thanks to the Babushka. The girl home and safe, the men cringing towards the harshness of the elderly woman, another act of kindness and protection from the only woman who seemed to care in the entire town of Klin. The Babushka removed herself from the town center once the girl made it across safely. The remainder of the day the old woman would safeguard the children walking home.

Every other day the young girl would visit her friend, every other day the girl would pass by the farm of Demitre. Every other day Demitre would be standing outside his farm waving hello to the girl. Demitre smitten by the girl and the girl had her crush on Demitre. Neither one of the two had courage to approach one another. Demitre dreamed of her as a wife, the girl dreamed of a white wedding. The young girl loved the Babushka for her caring. Demitre looked at the Babushka as a Good Samaritan who should mind her own business. The two at odds of their opinions, but who knew, they had only caught each other's eye once.

The west side of my home laid a stretch of road. In March it is a mixture of mud, ice, and horse manure. Constantly the rich citizens with their horse and buggies would fly by at amazing speeds. It was not hard to see an accident waiting to happen. During the school year the Babushka waits to help the children cross the road. In Klin it seems only the rich have somewhere to go. For example the widow who supports me. She has time for no one, only herself. Who am I to judge? I take what she gives and I am thankful. All my life I had to do what others have instructed, I still felt like a child in Moscow. The teachers applying pressure to complete a deadline. Daily the babushka continued her patriotic duty to Klin, and mother Russia. To the drunks she was a bother. To the children she was the local law enforcement. To the young girl she was a hero, to Demitre she was a nuisance, to the rich she was a rat, and to me she was a show.

One morning I awoke to another day. March was coming to an end and April approached. Occasionally snow would fall, only to give way to the sun, the air still crisp, the trees soon to bloom. This morning being like all others, for example morning tea, writing, look out my windows to see my show of the daily life in Klin. This afternoon my literary sponsor will come and read my latest story. A story written especially for the widows grandchildren. The Westside road continuing to be mud, ice, and manure, suddenly hearing a knock at the door, remaining in my study while the Mongolian servant escorts the rich widow, I stood behind my oak desk. My hands pressing the creases of my shirt and tie while the widow storms into the study without an announcement. "Where is the story?" Her hand out towards me, palm up. "Right here my lady." Placing the papers I held in my hand, giving them to the pompous woman. The widow scans my story with her wicked eye and no words, until. "Very good, I shall send a note of payment promptly with another month free rent." Bowing to the widow slightly, "Thank you my lady." The rich woman dressed in black saunters out of the study. Walking over to my window overlooking the street filled with horses and carriages I look out the window to observe my meal ticket climbing into her black carriage with her white pristine horses. Her driver lending her a hand, the carriage leaning towards the street while her weight shifted the carriage.

With cup and saucer in hand, feeling the saucer slip from my left hand a tear falling to the ground, my tears. What I witnessed changed my life forever; this small town that imprisons me became my eternal nightmare, my hell. The carriage of the rich woman speeding off onto the western street, the white horses in full galloping stride while in the middle of the street the Babushka holding the hand of a child. The old woman doing her usual duty for the community while the young girl of Demitre's heart sees the old woman and child, realizing the rushing carriage and the possible tragedy.

The young girl runs out to the Babushka with child. Demitre who was following the young girl with his eyes, now realizing. The child, Babushka, the young girl, all in the path of the oncoming carriage, in haste and without thinking he rushes out to rescue his secret love. The driver of the carriage not paying attention to the road before him while Demitre grabs the young girl by the shoulder as she turns to face him, their eyes meet. They knew at that moment their secret love was mutual. Before a word could be spoken four lives snuffed out of existence.

The carriage running over the Babushka and the child causing the carriage to lean left from the impact rolling over the bodies, the carriage slamming into Demitre and the young girl, it was all a sudden blur but it also seemed to all be moving in slow motion. The second impact and the trampling of the four bodies sent the rich woman's carriage into a ditch. The wheels unhinged and separating from the carriage, the driver killed instantly. The carriage rolling and tumbling into the ditch, the driver's body crushed, the rich woman who bought my story, dead. Her elderly body not able to take the impact as it rolled around inside the carriage like a child doll. The town of Klin fell into silence, not even the birds made a sound. Six lives gone in a single moment, tears streamed down my face, the town people surrounded the scene. I could no longer witness the sorrowful event, walking to my desk, placing the tea cup next to my quills. I stood in silence.

I could not write for months, I had not the courage. For a time without the Babushka Klin became a place controlled by the drunks, the mob. Until one early morning in December I heard a familiar voice on the streets of Klin. It was another Babushka.

Smiling lightly I sat at my desk and placed my quill in hand, inspired to write again. On the title page I wrote "The Mighty Babushka."

FIN.

(The story written in Russia, March 2010)

The Eye of Devastation

By Davidson L. Haworth

In this world of corruption and arrogance there is a lone image that haunts me in my sleep. Eight months ago while I walked the dark dank alleys of Moscow I first saw this image. I was not alone this night while under my arm was a local girl. Like most Russian girls she was beautiful with long flowing brunette hair, and blazing blue eyes. Her image would shock any American male into instant submission. Her curves mesmerized even for the most experienced man in regards to the opposite sex.

This night we spent the cold winter evening in a local bar drinking vodka and wine, feeling the warm heat from the fireplace adjacent to our table with a single white candle. Outside the snow fell from heaven lightly upon the Moscow walkways. Looking outside the window people walked covered in their warmest clothes and scurrying along. The night was still young and I wanted to walk to Pushkin square to take in the snowfall upon my face. My Russian companion would have none of my ideas and demanded to take the Moscow metro to her apartment. She was eager to bring me to her abode and settle in for a night of romantic exploits.

The young girl and I walked towards the metro, the sound of the snow upon the ground being crushed by our black boots. Entering the metro the warm air suddenly hits my face while homeless people huddle in the corners keeping warm, and Babushkas, young wannabe gangsters walking through the metro. The Moscow police looking at me with a slight hesitation and I knew their thoughts, a westerner with another one of their girls. It is something they see on a daily basis, nothing new to them. Moscow is quite worldly and the police know the score. The sounds of the metro trains rushing by the platforms while the cool air being felt from within the metro tunnel. My young companion tugged my hand, her way of instructing me to jump onto the fully loaded metro. She continued to tug like a child wanting a Mother's attention. There was something in the metro that caught my eye. I was shocked and blinded by the image that surrounded my soul and made me a prisoner.

A young girl at the end of the metro, her back against the wall, clothes worn, boots torn, face marred with misery. I walked closer to her while my companion gave a look of disappointment. Closer I moved to the girl of misery, in her hands a sign. Turning to my lovely girl I asked, "What does the sign say?" My Russian beauty paused and answered my query. "It says please help me get a new eye." I turned to my girl and then back to the girl holding the sign, and then I noticed. She only had one eye and no patch covering the missing eye. I stared into the nonexistence of the missing eye. Blackness and darkness over took me.

My companion noticed my shock and said, "She is the victim of the mafia. She sits here all day with a sign wanting money to fix her eye. The end of the day the mafia picks her up and they take majority of her earnings." The beautiful girl shrugs her shoulders and continues, "Its Russian life. It is what it is." I could not move, the beautiful girl guiding me to the next metro on the other side of the platform doing her best to guide me through the crowd of people. The rest of the night the thought of the one eyed girl haunted my senses.

From that day the girl with one eye haunted me. Her image enters my dreams and at times while I walk in the darkness of night I see her eye. Her missing eye watching me and in the shadows I can feel the eyes follow me. The girl with the eye of devastation affecting everyone who glares upon her with their own eyes, haunted by her we all remain scarred for life. Somewhere in the metro or the dark streets of Moscow the girl walks. She is out there somewhere devastating everyone who looks upon her. Her eyes following us till the end of our lives on earth.

October 23, 2010

Your Time Will Come

A Short Story
By
Davidson L. Haworth

San Francisco, California, a young foreign exchange student from Germany named Armin Fassbinder, sits over looking the grounds of San Francisco University. The moon shining from above, a light glow piercing through the dorm window, his room in complete darkness, except for his computer monitor screen. The blue glow shining upon Armin's young adolescent face, he dreamed of one day coming to the United States, obsessed with Hollywood films and McDonalds. He had grown up wanting to live the life he found so fascinating in films. His parents did not prefer his taste in American culture, hence his secret obsession shared between his younger sister and himself.

His steady hands froze while the sound of typing ceased. Placing his hand upon his stomach, he was hungry and thought of going out for one of his late night American crap food binge eating sessions. He rose from his desk and left his computer on with a high energy track playing. Walking to his closet he pulls out his university sweat shirt leaving his dorm with his wallet in his back pocket.

The street bustling this Friday evening and every Friday in the city while young girls dressed like hookers, drug dealers, homeless, all mingle together like human debris in a dumpster. In the distance Armin can see the golden arches of his favorite fast food joint. Suddenly his smile turns to a look of despair, and then darkness surrounded him, silence. His blood slowly flowing between the cracks of the pavement, two men wearing black hoods running from the scene, the student's lifeless body ignored by the passersby, Armin another victim of the American streets, a boy with a bright future extinguished forever. His time had come and gone, and eventually your time will come.

The Last Grizzly

By Davidson L. Haworth

T he formidable Grizzly Bear ruled the western United States and Canada. During the 1800's European settlers came to California in droves to strike it rich in the gold rush. From England to Germany, New York, and Montreal, all traveled to make their claim. In this time of greed and arrogance the grizzly bear stood against the settlers and in the end lost. Settlers who could not make it rich panning for gold and turned to other get rich quick schemes in the golden state. Some even went as far as becoming fur traders. For years the grizzly fought against human expansion and the settlers fought for gold; furs, oil, and superiority of the land. Eventually the settlers would win the fight for supremacy and the grizzly would hide for fear of extinction.

Several years pass and California gradually becomes civilized. Gone are the Gunslingers and Pioneers, a new era in state history has erupted. Living in a small town in Fresno County a young girl named Polly, her blonde hair and freckled face is the charm of Fresno. Her proper lady like demeanor surprised many of the citizens of her small beloved town of Fresno. The town is becoming populated with immigrants from all over the world and Americans traveling from the east coast. Though California lost the gold rush the people still came from all over the country and the world to live in the wonderful sunshine of the golden state.

The twelve year old Polly adored the stories of the pioneers of old and the adventures. Sitting on her wooden porch with a book in hand she hears footsteps approaching. Suddenly she hears a familiar voice, the voice of her neighbor. "What are you reading Polly?" The young girl sitting upon the porch raises her head and answers. "My dear Anna I am reading a classic tale of responsibility called The Hiltons' Holiday, written by a Sarah Orne Jewett. I find the story to be charming and endearing. Have you read this story Anna?" The neighbor girl frowns and says with sorrow. "Unfortunately not, my father is forcing the writings of Homer upon me." Polly joins her friend in her sorrow until she invites her to spend time with her on the porch. The two girls take turns reading the story together, reading one paragraph at a time.

Suddenly the girls are startled by the sound of a horn, a car horn to be exact. The girl's mouths drop to the ground while the car stops in front of Polly's home. Out of the car comes her father Herbert Chesterfield. A round portly fellow with a clean cut appearance and a smile that was the talk of Fresno. "Greetings Anna and Polly, what do you think of my new acquisition?" Polly's father speaking to the girls with a sense of pride and accomplishment, his daughter stands from her seated position on the porch, while her friend follows her lead. With amazement the girl speaks to her father while she and her companion approach the car. "Father where did you find this car, or did you borrow it from one of your friends?" Herbert glides his hand across the fender of the car and says with pride. "No my dear Polly this car belongs to us now. I just purchased it." The young studies the car with her eyes and says to her father. "I guess black is the only color?" Herbert laughs responding. "Yes for now that is all we have here unless you live in Los Angeles. The car is called a Ford model T center door sedan, perfect for travel. Maybe if you're good I will take you and Anna fishing this weekend." Polly smiled and said. "Sorry papa but there is a celebrity coming into town and he peaks my curiosity. He is known to be an explorer of the Sierra Mountains and a bit of a legend. I will take a rain check on your invite though." Polly giving her Father an innocent smile. "Very well Polly, I will wait for your company and we shall bring a picnic basket." The young girl was becoming impulsive and wanted the weekend to approach; her thoughts were on the visiting adventurer.

The weekend finally arrived with a week full of homework and weekday obstacles, now the two girls were ready for the appearance of the great adventurer, and the girls were the first to arrive to the town hall. Slowly people began to arrive and the town workers placed balloons and a large sign welcoming the visitor. The sign read in bold red lettering "Welcome to Fresno Charles Klondike!" Polly in her best dress of white lace and pink flowers waited for this Mr. Klondike to arrive.

Finally the time had come and the mayor of Fresno "Truman C. Hart" began to speak. The mayor was a kind man who enjoyed being in the limelight and his introduction went on longer than Polly expected, until finally Mr. Klondike was introduced. Walking on the steps of Fresno town hall was none other than Charles Klondike. A rugged looking gentleman with a long beard and a beaver fur cap, his clothes looked like something from an old western. The young girl stood in amazement while Klondike spoke of his adventures throughout the mid-west until he said something Polly and Anna did not like. "I have come to Fresno, California on a hunt for the last grizzly in California." The people cheered on the adventurer while the two girls frowned, her admiration turned to sorrow and disgust. Polly loved all animals and always did what she could for them; she considered them angels walking upon the earth.

The two companions ran home to prepare for this Mr. Klondike and oppose his hunting expedition. Hours passed and Polly met her friend Anna near the town hall. The girls were dressed in high boots; tan trousers, buttoned up white shirts and pony tails. Suddenly they notice an old covered wagon from the 1800's appearing and park in front of the town hall. Town workers begin to load the wagon with bear traps and ammunition. Polly snaps her fingers and says to friend. "We will jump in the back of the wagon and hide, and then when the time is right we will stop Klondike from his mission." The two girls wait for an opportunity to climb in the wagon, eventually hiding themselves under a green tarp. The girls waited for some time and heard the voice of the adventurer, the wagon beginning to move. Charles Klondike traveled alone and entered the mountains of Tulare County.

The road was tough going for the girls, but once the wagon reached the final destination they jumped off and hid in the trees. They watched Charles Klondike while he set up traps and placed deer meat in the trees. The girls eventually set up a camp not far from Klondike; they wanted to spy on him constantly. No fire was ever set in their camp and food was scarce for the young girls. In the evening they would sneak into the camp of Klondike and take what was left over from his dinner, mixed with fresh berries they would find in the forest.

Four days passed and five nights came to an end, the sun now rising once more for a new day. In Fresno a hunt for the girls continued while missing person reports and Fresno's first radio station placed news spots on the missing girls. Polly and Anna hungry and prepared to give up hope suddenly heard a loud roar echoing through the deep mountains of California. Lifting themselves from the ground they ran towards the sound of the painful moaning of a bear. In Klondike's camp a large bear captured in his trap, the teeth of the trap ripping into the bear's leg, blood flowed readily. Polly turned to her friend and said. "Come let us try and rescue the grizzly." Anna looked at her friend in amazement and responded. "You must be out of your mind. That bear is at least 1500 pounds and 8 feet in height." Polly ignored the words of her friend and ran towards the grizzly. The girl only a few feet from the innocent victim hoping to rescue the grizzly from the trap, suddenly a shot rang out echoing loud and heard for miles. The grizzly falling to the ground in front of Polly, the back of the bears head decimated from the shot originating from behind. There beyond the bear stood Charles Klondike with a smile upon his face. The grizzly dead before the eyes of innocent Polly her tears form in her eyes, streaming down her cold cheeks.

Charles Klondike notices the girls and says. "What in the hell are you girls doing here?" Polly jumps up from the ground and charges Klondike. Charles wraps his arms around her while she hits and pounds on his chest. "How can you kill an innocent bear? How can you do this?" Tears flowing down the young girls face while Anna falls to the ground in tears. Klondike throws the innocent girl to the ground and says. "Easy my dear it is all about economics. I need money to live and this was a perfect way to make a name for myself, the one who killed the last grizzly." Eventually Klondike packed up his camp and his treasure while the girls knelt to the ground holding each other in tears of sorrow and pain. Klondike didn't even have the decency to report the girls hiding in the mountains once he reached Fresno. He gloated in his new fame and fortune.

Two years later Polly and Anna were camping with Herbert in the high Sierra's. The car was a great tool to pack up camping gear and make an enjoyable weekend. While on a hike Polly and Anna noticed in the distance a small grizzly bear. A smile came upon their faces, Polly finally saying to her friend. "Tell no one of this, it is our secret." From that day forward the girls told not a soul of their encounter for fear of hunters wanting fame. When Polly lay upon her death bed in the year 1982 in Raisin City, she told of the last grizzly in California.

Acknowledgments

T
he second book in this series has been a real joy in regards to doing historical research for some of the new characters and the people in my life who supported me in this great adventure are truly an inspiration in my life. First I want to thank my father Robin Haworth who helped form my appreciation for classical Tchaikovsky. If he did not expose me to such great composers I think my life would be much different and not as enriching, he was always there for me in my life and a great example of a father. My children who always stand by my side, Theo, Xavier, and Trinity, who's love and support keeps my drive alive to be the best that I can be in this world as a father and morally. Michael Haworth my brother and his two kids little Mike and Hope who are always in my prayers and thoughts. My mother in law Evgeniya Lukyantseva and Ludmila Lozbineva my wife's wonderful aunt who keeps me in line and focused on tasks in regards to writing about the motherland of Russia. Last but not least my wife whom this book is dedicated to. Her support is something unimaginable and never thought a human can possibly be so caring.

There are many people along the way who helped me last year coming to support me during the book tour and who spread the word about "The Dragon of Prali" throughout Europe and beyond. Pauli Lisibach, Mariann Martinsen, Magdalena Michniewska, Yadira

Salazar, Diana Andrade Andrade, Anna Goryacheva, Alessandro Mitillo, Angela Porter Shyock, Carma Spence and her podcast "The Genre Traveler," Anne Delaney SFO, Cyndi Davidson, Rick Cowan, Deanna Sillars, Debra Hallyburton, Eva Juhņēviča, George H-Freyre, Howard Lewelling III and his wonderful family, Julie Myers, Lynn Rudolph, Lynnette Gotthold-Stadmiller, Maria Kazanskaya, Tai Adelaja, Walter Lefeber, Astrid Samways. All these people I keep in my prayers and a big thank you. Last year I also spent loads of time promoting my works in the Russian Federation and a special thanks to the two Russian organizations who invited me to speak, American Center in Moscow and Chekhov Center.

There are family members and then there are cousins who help you along the way. I want to thank all my cousins from Massachusetts to Felixstowe, United Kingdom. Henry Bury, Clive Bury, Matthew Bury, James "Razz" Bury, Thomas Bury, Catherine Bury, Karin Bury, Carol Phillips, Sadie Scaggs, Jenifer Murphy, John Phillips, Marilyn King-Simoes, Michael Ogden, Martyn Ogden, Neal Ogden and his fantastic wife. Thank you all for the support and encouragement.

ILLUSTRATOR

Maria Andrade Andrade

Biography

Born in Astrakhan, Russia, in 1981, an artist and graphic designer with roots in Russia and Ecuador,

Having spent many years in Russia, Maria witnessed big historical events, such as the fall of the Soviet Union that gave many artists a chance to explore their individual talents.

Despite these political changes it wasn't until she visited her Ecuadorian father in his hometown Guayaquil, when Maria started to develop her painting skills. The bright colors of the Guayas region played a critical role in this evolution and formed her artistic style, colorful, vibrant and bright. To pursue her dream to become an artist Maria entered the Design and Drawing Faculty of Astrakhan University and successfully graduated in 2001.

Since 2006 Maria has been a member of the International Art Fund and participated in numerous exhibitions and contests around the world, including The 7th Annual Art Inter/National Exhibition at BoxHeart Expressions Gallery in Pittsburgh, PA, Manhattan Arts Gallery in New York, House of Artist in Moscow, Banca Monte dei Paschi di Sena Spa in Brussels and many others. Her paintings can be found in private collections in Russia, Belgium, Chile, Ecuador, Greece, Italy, Spain and USA.

Together with painting, Maria is also working on design projects and doing book covers and illustrations. She is the artist of the book covers for *The Dragon of Prali (2010)* and *The Wizard of Prali (2011)* by American writer Davidson L. Haworth.

You may find many of her works on her web site: http://www.andrade.ru/